The woman stopped four feet from Evil. Closer, her being an inch shorter didn't factor in. Something, maybe her authoritative tone, made her seem taller.

With her hand out, she ordered, "Ident." She sounded annoyed.

Slowly, Evil went to his front right pocket.

Since they weren't attacking him or arresting him, they were buying his cover. He dipped his hand in his pocket, pulled his wallet, and took out the real Ernest Smith's ident card. He placed it against the hacked government lo-jack transmitter on his neck, and—money well spent—the star-spangled glow of his holo-ident card presenting Ernest's information lit the side of his face.

A BOY NAMED EVIL, ULTRAHUMANS

An Ultrahumans short novel

EZEKIEL JAMES BOSTON

ELSEWHERE
E
P
PUBLISHING

A Boy Named Evil: Ultrahumans

Published 2017 by Elsewhere Publishing
www.ElsewherePublishing.com

ISBN-13: 978-1-62538-052-4

Elsewhere Publishing
www.ElsewherePublishing.com

Dedicated to:

Family & Friends
Mentors & Minions
Kay McGarvey

Ezekiel James Boston's
ULTRAHUMANS

A BOY NAMED EVIL

Chapter One

BEING ERNEST

"WELL." a woman with a husky voice called, "if it isn't Mr. Evil Overlord."

Though he hated being called by his name, Evil was well practiced at not reacting to hearing it. He lifted the thin metal lid to the industrial dumpster out behind Norwest Grind. A sour smell of milk turned bad wafted from the bin as he tossed in the two p.m. trash. While his insides shivered at the thought of his great-grandfather's lackeys finally finding him, Evil couldn't help but shake his head at the break in simple Norwest Grind procedure.

He used the smell, a recurring problem, as a means to stay in character as Ernest Smith Junior, the *son* part of the popular mother/son coffee shop.

No one wanted to take the trash out because of the smell. If everyone followed the simple procedure he had put in place of rinsing out the various empty milk and cream containers and bagging them properly, there wouldn't be a smell to contend with. Evil released the lid and let it bang closed.

"Salutations, E-vil." This gruff voice, a second one, was

male and sounded just like his great-grandfather's, but the words didn't have the suffocating telepathic heft.

Fully aware that the voices came from his right out toward the mouth of the alley that spilled into the strip mall's employee parking lot, Evil glanced left as though he had heard them from that way.

Per lease standards, the three sets of shops' gray-black back doors to the dead end left of him had their dumpsters and pallets pressed neatly against the walls. If need be, he had a totally clear path all the way to the gray-black back door of G14, the Army Surplus store that he owned through a shell company. While his great-grandfather would have dozens of ways of destroying the building in a blink of an eye—in which case he'd be totally screwed anyhow—the lackeys wouldn't.

Unless the orders had change, they were to bring him back alive. And, rightfully fearful of his great-grandfather's wrath, none of them would risk causing an iota of damage over what it would take to capture him.

Movement along the three-story roofline above G14 caught his attention. A rifleman in bulky SWAT style body armor had shifted to drop his cheek against his weapon and eye the scope.

Kicking into high gear, the inhibitor vest that Evil had purchased from Jimmy Alcazar warmed and thrummed softly against his chest under his long sleeve hunter-green Norwest Grind polo and yellow apron. Carrie Smith, the *mother* part of the coffee shop, was a proud Oregon Duck graduate and, as a luminary in the community, she incorporated the colors into her company, including hunter-green jeans and yellow vans.

Though mostly nerfed by his inhibitor, Evil's TA—his tactical awareness, the power that annoyed him the most—dimmed the world slightly to highlight the rifleman. Then, in an instant, five other riflemen were popped from the background. Because they were mostly blocked by the ledge, his power couldn't tell how tall the shooters were; but it noted their general shape for future indexing and advised their distance away.

While he couldn't help but notice the first one, he made no outward gesture to let on that he knew about the others.

Looking up at the rifleman, Evil raised his hands in the air with his fingers spread.

The riflemen were good news. The two speaking from the mouth of the alley weren't his great-grandfather's lackeys. All members of the Peacekeepers were too full of themselves and power-proud to make use of lowly riflemen, even when they would offer an overwhelming advantage. Like now.

Evil felt like he had missed something in his reaction. What else would a non-powered person do if they had a gun pointed at them? Was he supposed to cry? Babble for his life? Wet himself? His mind raced for the elusive answer.

The woman said, "Relax."

Familiar with the area, Evil's TA laid out the alley behind him with the four other stores to the mouth of the alley. The voice came from two feet inside the alley, precisely where she had originally called to him the first time.

Evil didn't relax. Though he'd missed something in his reaction, they hadn't noticed. He began to ease his way to the back door to Norwest Grind.

"Not so fast." The woman said, "Turn around."

Evil did. His TA lit them and the two Streit Cyclone SWAT vehicles that thundered in to block the alley.

Eighty-five feet away, both the woman, 5'6" and curvaceous in the ways that made Evil's teenage mind take note, and the skinny 5'11" man were decked out in full black tactical gear. Though their armor looked like typical SWAT armor, they had black visors over their eyes and they didn't have weapons of any sort.

If they were non-powered in full gear, they'd have

weapons on their hips or, like the riflemen above, have the gun butts against their shoulders. Their lack of typical weapons screamed that they both had some sort of projectile power: laser beams, ice shards, kinetic blasts; something.

Both of them started to close on him. While the woman was more business, on a direct path, the man sort of sauntered along, lagging back just a touch.

The woman stopped four feet from Evil. Closer, her being an inch shorter didn't factor in. Something, maybe her authoritative tone, made her seem taller.

With her hand out, she ordered, "Ident." She sounded annoyed.

Slowly, Evil went to his front right pocket.

Since they weren't attacking him or arresting him, they were buying his cover. He dipped his hand in his pocket, pulled his wallet, and took out the real Ernest Smith's ident card. He placed it against the hacked government lo-jack transmitter on his neck, and—money well spent—the star-spangled glow of his holo-ident card presenting Ernest's information lit the side of his face.

Reading, she took a step back.

The guy finally made it to stand next to her. He raised his visor, revealing pale skin and eyes slightly obscured by brown mist. A telltale power indicator. Evil had seen similar effects before, but the abilities range from powerful eye beams to inoffensive air purification. Since only a couple of the Power League's front men and leaders went without masks, the mist wasn't enough to nail down an identity.

Focusing on his face, Brown Mist said, "Ernest Smith. J. R." He glanced at the projected info and then split his focus between the corners of Evil's eyes and the corners of his mouth, the usual glitch spots of—illegal for non-costume—falseface overlays. "Where were you last night?"

"Kyoto, Japan." Evil answered without hesitation. Jimmy

Alcazar's falseface was better than anything available to most. This would test just how good.

The real Ernest Smith loved jet-setting and, as part of the deal of Evil taking over the humdrum everyday aspects of Ernest's life, frequently updated his journal in a private cloud server. A journal Evil read often and occasionally left notes in. Evil's entries were usually short, advising Ernest of what was being done in his absence. A few times Evil prompted Ernest to call his mom; those prompts always came after she dropped a surprise visit on the Norwest Grind that Ernest typically worked out of and Evil had left her standing there.

Evil said, "I was at the opening of the first Norwest Grind in Kyoto Station." Making sure to keep his tone respectful, he asked, "Why?"

The woman grumbled. "It's legit."

Thrilled, Evil kept his emotions in check.

She turned to Brown Mist and whispered, "Damn it. Another false lead." She stalked away and spoke at her wrist. "Roof and perimeter teams. Stand down." Though it looked like she was holding back her anger, she hauled off and kicked a dumpster. The industrial bin whined as it buckled and slammed into the wall.

Evil jumped at both sounds. Nerfed, his TA couldn't hone in on exactly who she was from her body and gait, but the kick narrowed her identity down to three Power League brawlers: Peach, Viper, or Granite. This kind of operation—not to mention the all-black uniform—wasn't Peach's style, and Viper always seemed too in control of herself to allow that kind of lashing out. Though it could be any one of the three, Granite was the odds-on favorite.

"This is a little embarrassing." Though Brown Mist still kept a sharp eye for a glitch, his voice took on a modest tone. "We had intel that one of the company employees here is wanted."

The guy had worded his accusation carefully. He didn't say, *we heard you were the great-grandson of Supreme—the most powerful ultrahuman on the planet, grandson of Ultimate—a villain the world never got to appreciate, and son of Perfection—the man who nearly eradicated everyone of Chinese decent by targeting markers in their DNA with genetically modified food.* The guy also didn't say *I believe you're innocent and you're free to go.*

Though Evil's false identity wasn't meant to hide from the Power League, he swallowed in relief. It was strong enough to stand up to their scrutiny. Jimmy truly was a genius.

"Well." Evil put the ident card back in his wallet and the wallet back in his pocket. "If it'll help, I can call everyone in so that you can interview them."

"No, thanks." Brown Mist shook his head. The mist that obscured his eyes faded, showing earth-brown irises. "The guy we're after comes from a line of real bad news. So, sorry about all of this..." He motioned to the riflemen along the roof and the SWAT vehicles. "And for taking up your time."

Evil understood that his great-grandfather wanted him back under control, but he hadn't done anything to anyone to warrant the Power League coming after him.

Grasping for understanding as to why he was wanted, Evil asked, "If I may, what'd the guy you're after do?"

"Nothing." Brown Mist's shrug looked weird through the SWAT armor. "At least not yet."

"Oh." Evil frowned as he fought the logical follow up question of, *then why are you after him?* He felt as though he had asked the one question that someone who is not used to seeing a show of force would ask. One of the many things his training had taught him was that looking—being—too composed was as much of a flag as asking too many questions.

Granite raised her arm at the SWAT vehicles and wound her hand in some circles.

The vehicles crept back.

Brown Mist turned to leave and turned back. He motioned to the mangled dumpster. "Hey, tell your landlord that he'll be getting a check from the League about that."

Evil nodded. "Will do."

"Thanks." The guy extended his hand.

Evil's nerfed TA alerted him that the guy had removed his tactical glove a split second before their hands made contact.

They shook hands.

Brown Mist's grip seized up and clamped hard. His jaw locked. His eyes glossed over with inky black. Soft pleading groans worked in his straining neck.

Evil whispered, "Shit." He grabbed onto the guy's thumb with his other hand and worked to get free.

If it had been just a regular handshake, nothing would've happened. It would've just been a typical parting gesture that Evil had done countless times since he and his mother fled their home country that his great-grandfather controlled.

However, the guy had to have tried to do something sneaky, a mental or emotional trick of some sort, to be ensnared by the psychic trap that was woven into Evil's psyche by Tar—his father's top mentalist—before evil had uttered his first word.

Focusing, Evil struggled against the confining mental yoke from the inhibitor that made it feel like someone had slipped his powers a pill that put them in a constant coming-out-of-a-coma stupor; which, originally, was the plan. He had worked with Jimmy to make the design stronger and had willingly put it on. His powers were a link, a legacy, to his father's side of the family and Evil wanted nothing to do with them. But right now—

Right now, Evil summoned every iota of mental control that he could muster. Hoping it would be enough, Evil looked the guy in his blackened eyes and quietly ordered, "Let. Go."

Chapter Two

FIGHTING TO STAY FREE

THE ALLEY behind Norwest Grind rocked side to side.

No.

It was still. Nothing had moved at all.

But it sure as hell felt like the earth had just rocked back and forth. Not enough to take your feet from under you, but strong enough to nearly make you swoon.

Filling Evil's nose and mouth, the spoiled cream smell from the dumpster intensified. His stomach lurched as though he had decided to chug a quart of expired milk. Breathing—his, Brown Mist's, Granite's, and the riflemen on the roof—roared like double-hauling big rigs tearing down the highway.

Brown Mist's eyes widened and the blackness budged outward to form oblong balloons stretching to make contact with Evil eyes.

This wasn't real.

Couldn't be real.

This was just like the time when Evil's dad had told him to try and read him when he was four. It was the first time Evil had experienced true terror. The worst thing his four-year-old mind could imagine—his dad abandoning him at the beach with faceless, dog-headed strangers with lobster claw hands—had held him fast.

His father said that he had only waited a few seconds before pulling little Evil out of Tar's trap; banishing the terror that haunted his nightmares for years. A nightmare that, after a stressful day, would still drop by to make the night insufferable.

No!

Evil yanked to get his hands free. Though ten years older, he knew much more about the world, how it worked, and didn't want any part of the kind of horrors that waited for him in Tar's trap.

Brown Mist's fingers were like gas-powered pistons holding Evil in place.

Not only had his mental command to make the guy let go not work, but—somehow—it had caused some sort of feedback loop in the trap that worked to reach out to him. To grab him. To pull him in.

No!

Evil leaned back.

The blackness in the man's eyes took on pincer-like appendages that snapped at him.

Held in place, Evil dodged.

Left.

Right.

He kneed Brown Mist in the junk.

The guy's hand popped open.

The alley snapped back to normal. No wobbling. No horrendous taste or stench. No whooshing breath. Just the steady ground that the earth—barring earthquakes—always provided. That and the slight whiff of bad cream in the air, and the revving of the Streit Cyclones as they trundled backward.

Granite, who had been motioning the trucks to back up was still doing that motion.

It had only been a split second.

Black tears, a thick morass, dangled from Brown Mist's eyes to his cheeks. Reacting in slow motion to whatever tormented him the most, his brow knotted behind his knitted ski mask and his mouth began to open. He'd start wailing soon.

When Evil's TA was at full strength, it would let him know paths to take, the best moves to make; it'd optimize everything for him over the next few minutes to give him the best chance of success. Nerfed, it could only make him vaguely aware of threats. For the first time in his life, it was up to him to figure out the best move.

About to head back into Norwest Grind, his TA flashed four faces of customers—new customers—who had been in the lounge drinking coffee for hours; not quite fitting in, but not standing out enough to make Evil think twice about their prolonged presence. At least, not until his TA flashed their faces.

He didn't know who they were, but they would play some part if he went back in.

Casually, Evil walked toward G14 at the end of the alley.

Running would alert the riflemen.

It was best to act as if all was normal until Brown Mist started wailing. Then, all bets would be off.

Evil passed the first set of doors. Two more.

Granite said, "Come on, Dreamweaver, let's load up."

Evil's eyes widened. Dreamweaver was a world-class psychometrist. While not in the Power League proper, Dreamweaver often freelanced for them and law enforcement—and anyone with the dough—to help find whoever they paid him to find.

Passing the second set of doors, Evil pulled his phone,

typed 777 and hashtag. The pre-programmed code sent a message to Ernest Smith Junior alerting him that the jig was up and that he should immediately enact the fallout plan. In three days the plan would give Evil a bad reputation, but it would leave Ernest and Carrie Smith with plausible deniability instead of dragging them into being complicit in helping him, which shouldn't have been a crime but—because of his legacy—probably would be.

"Dream?" Granite said, "Come on. Wheels up."

Evil passed the next set of doors. One more set and he'd be one last length away from slipping free.

"Hey, Ernest." Suspicion slipped into Granite's voice, "Where you goin'?"

A gut-wrench jagged yell filled the alley. Freed from the molasses of his mind, Dreamweaver let loose with one after another after another.

Now! Feet pounding the ground, Evil sprinted past the last set of doors.

"Shoot!" Granite yelled, "Take him down!"

Evil's TA alerted him to the movement above. Nerfed, his powers didn't tell him anything else. There was nothing he could do but run harder.

Muffled gunfire rang out.

The pale, electric-blue pinpoint forcefield that he had built into the inhibitor vest flashed around him.

Rubber bullets thumped around him.

Ahead, the six deadbolts and lever locks on G14's back door clacked and unlocked in rapid succession. The sensors picked up on his proximity. Good. Money well spent. The door flew open.

A deep, baleful wail closed in fast behind Evil.

Hoping to dodge what he figured was a speedster, Evil dashed sideways.

Something large and green sucked wind as it whistled

past. It slammed into the reinforced doorjamb and wall with the cry of twisting metal.

An industrial trash bin, one bent out of shape from a super-strength kick and throw, blocked his way into G14.

Eyeing an emergency ladder, Evil used his momentum to launch from pallets to the top of the upright garbage bin, and leapt for the bottom rung.

Used to moving faster and being stronger, his legs didn't even take him halfway.

His forcefield flashed as he bumped into the cinderblock wall and fell in the corner.

The gunfire stopped.

Dreamweaver's wailing continued.

Evil popped up to his feet.

Feet thumping hard on the ground, fists balled, Granite sprinted at him.

One of the riflemen yelled, "Kick his ass!"

Evil got some distance from the wall and put his fists up. Studying hero combat was a must and he knew Granite—with her superior body armor—tended to fight a little sloppy and favored headshots.

Her right fist came at his jaw with deadly intentions.

Evil ducked and swept her lead foot.

Reeking of cigarette smoke, she sailed past him and slammed into the wall, shattering a body-sized hole in it.

That was nothing. She'd be back on her feet in a moment.

Evil tore off back the way he'd come.

Dreamweaver was on his knees and arched back with his hands on the sides of his head.

Evil passed the first set of back doors.

The two SWAT vehicles rolled back into position to block the alley.

From over the top of them, a svelte woman—in the same black tactical gear—came flipping into the alley. She could be any one of a dozen on the Power League's roster. In each hand she held short, stubby chunks of gray metal, probably high-powered Tasers. If they weren't Tasers, it'd be best to take them on the inhibitor vest for maximum protection.

Evil's TA advised him that this was a losing fight. Whoever she was, she was quick and technical. She had perfect form and wasted zero energy as she ran at him.

An angry grunt came from behind him.

The woman in front of him jumped to the wall to spring high.

Giving up speed, Evil dodged low in the same direction.

The twisted, green bin whiffed by. It smashed into one of the SWAT vehicles, knocking it back a few feet. Evil eyed the small opening. Just enough space for him to slip out. He just had to get past the woman in front of him.

They ran toward each other.

Another grunt lit the air.

The woman stopped short, pivoted, and leapt left.

Not as nimble, Evil dove the same way.

Another garbage bin whistled past to crash at the mouth of the alley.

Evil popped up to his feet.

The woman slapped a chunk of metal onto his chest, knocking him backward.

His forcefield flashed brilliantly and faded.

Evil rolled back over his shoulder and got on his feet.

She had already launched herself at him and punched her other chuck of metal onto the first.

Knocked from his feet again, a vibrating warmth filled Evil's body and the world flashed a familiar gray.

A bright, gunmetal gray.

A teleportation gray.

A goodnight gray.

Chapter Three

THE DREAM IS OVER

EVIL'S MOUTH FELT, and tasted, like he'd bit into a warm, soft pretzel. Heck, he could even smell it. God he loved that taste. It tasted like freedom and fun.

It took his mind back a couple of years when his mom had taken him to the Ponderosa Ranch amusement park as an early twelfth birthday present. Though all the colorful commercials he had seen made him curious, he had protested when they actually went because of the volume of people there. However, due to the ravenous cheers inside the park, it didn't take much for his mom to overcome his reluctance.

They had been out of Primazone for a little over a month and his mom thought it was time for him to experience something typical for his age, for once, instead of the constant grooming to take over his great-grandfather's country. Right inside the front gates, she had bought him a warm pretzel and that first bite was oh, so good and—

The left side of his face lit with pain.

Someone had slapped him, hard.

Evil's eyes sprung open.

Framed by a cloud-strewn, bright blue sky, a sinewy man

with a hard face leaned over Evil and stared down at him. "Yup." The guy stood upright and said, "He's still alive."

On his back on the ground, Evil gazed at the guy, the guy's black military fatigues, and the guy's modified Desert Eagle sidearm. He then looked around to see that he was surrounded by twenty men dressed similarly, all looking to be in decent shape. They wore ski masks and had assault weapons: fifteen held AR-15s with the single-shot grenade launcher attachment, the other four held some modified version of an M32 grenade launcher with a larger, longer drum.

While none of them had their weapons pointed directly at him, they were all in a readied stance although the AR-15s had their safeties on. It wouldn't take much movement from them to flick the safeties off and put him down-barrel, which should've been enough to trigger his weakened TA to highlight them but it didn't.

His vest vibrated against him. The woman must've overclocked his vest somehow.

First time ever. Evil blinked impotently.

"You must be Evil Overlord." Slappy, the one who'd slapped him sized him up. "Not what I imagined. On your feet, asshole."

Not handcuffed or restrained, Evil stood.

The earth around them was mostly rocky dirt with large patches of yellowed crabgrass. Shrubs—winterfat, four-wing saltbush, and sagebrush—peppered the landscape. Rocky hills lined the horizon to the north and east while the land stretched forever out to the south and west.

Evil looked down at his chest. The two metal stubs remained stacked there on his apron at the center of his chest. Between the post-'port taste in his mouth and seeing them together, Evil felt an odd sense of honor. Before now, teleportation was only possible by people with the power or the huge sanctioned port stations. Someone had taken the spatial distorters and found a way to make them work on a personal level. World-changing technology created to capture him. And, perhaps of note for Jimmy, a way to strengthen the dampening vest.

One of the guys with an M32, with boulders for shoulders and massive biceps—the largest of the lot—said, "Huh. I thought he'd be younger. And, you know, black. Like his pops."

"It's probably a falseface." One of the thin guys, shorter than the rest—around Evil's own 5'7", but short for a grown man in this line of work—with an AR-15 shrugged his shoulder strap closer to his narrow neck. "Peel it off and I bet you he blackens to be just like the old man."

Evil tried to control his facial expressions, but his anger showed when his jaw tightened. He managed to keep his silence, though. As much as he wanted to apply the lessons of compassion and understanding that his mother had been sneaking him since they were introduced on his fifth birthday, everything about this situation made him pull on the teachings from his father and great-grandfather.

Keep a level head. Listen. And only speak when silence won't be accepted. They wanted him. They had him. He wasn't going to give them the pleasure of asking *what now*.

Boulder Shoulders said, "But the capture reports said he didn't use any powers. Maybe he don't got any."

Shorty blurted, "Ha! The descendant of the most powerful ultrahuman on the planet is a total dud."

That got a chuckle from the group.

Reflexively, Evil tensed and his fist balled. An ingrained pride in his powers and true power level almost broke through the last couple years of non-powered living. Then his mind hooked on the word *dud*. Non-powered people thought in binary powered and non-powered terms. Only power-proud people called normal people duds. So, did they all have powers or just the little guy?

"Quiet." Slappy read something in Evil's reaction. He glared at the two who had chattered, and pulled out a pair of dark violet sunglasses to point northeast with them.

The men there parted.

"We're heading that way." Slappy flicked the shades open and put them on. "Start walkin'."

Evil's mother had said—and shown him—that the world was a kinder place than his father made it out to be. The Power League and their colorful uniforms were a part of his mother's world. The people who attacked in the alley, and these twenty-one men, belonged to a part of the world that his father had warned him about. The part that would end him because of his lineage.

But they hadn't killed him. Yet. And thought he was powerless. Unless they tried the former, he wasn't going to disable his inhibitor vest to disprove the latter.

He started walking the way Slappy pointed. How many miles lay before him? The rocks in the dirt already bulged through his thin-soled Vans.

The men's boots crunched on the ground as they fanned out behind him. While tolerable for now, it'd be nice if they happened to have a spare pair of the tac boots in size ten.

Evil thought about his high-probability pending death. It could happen. If they did it fast, before he could disable the vest. Since his great-grandfather wasn't here to stop it, there was a good chance that they wouldn't kill him. However, Evil figured it was more likely that this group—if he were murdered by them—wouldn't take credit for it. His death may not be known for decades, if ever.

It was a closely kept secret that his great-grandfather had a cabal of upper echelon precogs actively monitoring future news and information hubs. There job was to search for any blips that didn't auto-trigger their power and would displease his great-grandfather. While they had a secret force at their command and acted autonomously on smaller stuff, they brought the big deals to his great-grandfather's attention. Evil wanted to believe his death—if known—would register.

Evil kicked a small rock. It tumbled along to dirt into a sagebrush. A tiny lizard skittered out and scurried away. Scared, but free.

There was great speculation of his great-grandfather being a precog when he miraculously showed up at the proclaimed secret location from where his father had broadcast to the world that he had set in motion the extermination of the Chinese, that it could only be undone by him, and he would only do that if Evil and his mother were turned over to him.

It sounded like a big gun pointed at the world's head. But Evil understood his father better than anyone else. What he was truly doing was casting as wide a net as possible to kill Evil's mother for stealing Evil away and not returning him. His father wanted her dead, even if he had to kill off every Chinese person to do it.

A faint roar of engines came from way high up and behind them. Still walking forward, he glanced back to the sky beyond the armed men behind him.

Above the clouds, a commercial plane flew from the south heading west by northwest.

Gaining the power of flight when he was eight had been awesome. Evil never thought his father, who always wanted him close and manageable, would ever allow him to gain—and keep—a power that would grant him a modicum of freedom. However, when Deborah Gilmore, a single-trick ultrahuman who barely qualified for citizenship, had tried to betray Primazone, her execution had been scheduled. And, of course, they weren't just going to allow her powers to slide into the ether to manifest in someone else. However, instead of absorbing her energy himself, Evil's father had used her to train Evil how to pull power into himself.

Because of his mother's teaching, Evil no longer felt a thrill when thinking back on Deborah's tan skin, blonde hair, and fierce blue eyes fading to chalk white as he syphoned her power. While he didn't believe his mom was a hundred percent right in her absolute assessment that stealing powers and murdering is always wrong, she had given him insight into being on the other side of the syphon; and—while occasionally necessary—it wasn't something to revel in. And neither was murder.

Evil walked close to a tall bunch of flowering four-wing saltbush to take in the tart perfume. His mother had said to appreciate the small things in life, which seemed silly at the time, but—for some reason—seemed apropos as he marched toward possible death.

He glanced at the men. They were still back there at firing squad distance. Keeping the same plodding pace.

As though it were why he turned, Evil looked to the plane farther along its flight path. It'd been so long since he felt the crisp cold air of speed at high altitudes on his face that he no longer missed it.

The thought brought bits of Deborah to mind. Her excitement over having a power manifest in her, the pure joy of being able to fly, and the thrill she felt when she pushed hard enough to finally break the hundred-miles-an-hour mark. While not all that fast for those with flight, she possessed unmatched maneuverability. Deborah was nowhere near their level, but she had had dreams of joining the Power League and choosing the moniker Hummingbird.

Evil knew those dreams because Deborah defined herself by the power. He tapped on her training memories often as he used his newly gained flight constantly for a few months, but the flight got old. Unless Evil needed to be somewhere in

Ultrava—Primazone's capital city—quicker than his feet would take him, he pretty much had stopped using it. There was usually a moment when the fraction of the person that came with the power faded and then the power was truly his, but what remained of Deborah still hung around.

His mother had called what Evil's father made him do to Deborah a *shame*. It was the first time he had heard the word, but her tone had clued him in to what it meant and how he should feel.

Evil dropped his gaze to the dirt a few feet ahead of him. He never told his mother that he used to beg for the chance to absorb others' powers before then.

It had taken his mother repeatedly talking about how syphoning powers was a disgrace and lecturing about the indignity of it for the lesson to take root. And, right now, that flash of Deborah, vibrant and alive in the skies, drove the point into his heart.

His father would've chastised him for allowing regret at taking her power take hold of him. They were superior and better than that. It was her decisions and actions that put her in the position to have her power syphoned. Further, she had proven that she wasn't worthy of powers the moment she acted against the oath she swore to his great-grandfather in order to become a Primazone citizen.

Still, in this case, Evil felt his mother was right. He didn't want to think about what his father would do to him for letting the soft regret totter into sorrow.

A distant whine of electric engines came from ahead.

Four desert camo Humvees were coming his way.

Evil slowed and glanced behind him.

The men also slowed. Their weapons remained at rest. So, the Humvees weren't an unwelcomed sight to them.

His feet were beginning to ache, and since he wasn't told to speed back up, Evil came to a complete stop.

So did the men.

Curling and uncurling his toes in his shoes, Evil put his hands on his waist and rested his thumbs on the vest's release levers. If this was where it was going to go down, he would power off the vest and only kill as many as he had to in order to get away. If the vest would come off...

Waiting for the Humvees, Evil perked his ears for the sound of even one click of a safety flicking off.

Chapter Four

AMERICA VS. PRIMAZONE LIVING

EACH HUMVEE HAD a long barrel machine gun on top, too big to be a simple .50 cal. The fact that the weapons were unmanned made Evil narrow his eyes in speculation. With the men armed behind him, it didn't make sense for the mounted weapons to not have hands on them. Perhaps they were controlled from within the vehicle.

The Humvees' large, reinforced tires crunching on the rocky dirt was the only sound giving away their approach. As they rolled to a stop, the engines gave a slight electric whine-down no louder than a Prius, which was as unnatural as the guns not being manned. All vehicles in Ultrava were electric, but—over the last two years—Evil had grown used to the sound of fossil fueled engines.

One of the drivers, in all black and a ski mask like the others, leaned out his window. "Uh, I'll take a large double caf with a marionberry scone."

Evil smiled and his shoulders hitched to laugh. He instantly stamped the surprised mirth down.

That was unexpected. The guy sounded every bit like a

regular Norwest Grind customer, particularly the marionberry scone.

Most of the armed men behind Evil chuckled. On the whole, these guys weren't all brass and balls. Some of them had jokes. Jokes that would've gotten them reprimanded in Primazone for not giving the situation the strict attention needed in the moment. Joking could be done after the situation was handled and resolved.

Maybe they thought he was handled.

The driver dropped back into his seat with a confused twist to his mouth before lipping, *he smiled?*

"This way." Slappy passed Evil and spun to not present his back. He walked backward toward the back of the Humvees.

What was this? Were they going to have him ride in it with them? Finding out that the people arrested by American police officers rode in the back of their squad cars, only separated by mesh, had thrown Evil for a loop. Sure, the perpetrator was in custody, but they could hear everything that went across the radios and interact. Possibly even employ sly psychology.

Slappy kept going past the rear doors.

Evil followed.

No longer in front of the vehicle that had stopped before him, the six by ten foot armored trailer hooked onto the back became visible. It had big Humvee tires that made the inset trailer tapered liked a stepside truck.

Okay. This made sense. This is how they transported fugitives in Primazone.

In fact, everything wrong with today felt like Primazone living. From the first group cornering him in an alley through now. Only in his native land, there wouldn't have been any hesitation or conversation. He would've been taken down swiftly and kept unconscious—either by telepathy or force—until fully restrained in the penitentiary.

Only the casual-ish way these men went about their jobs kept Evil from being one hundred percent sure that that last two years weren't an elaborate scenario that his great-grandfather used to test their citizens' loyalty and that Evil's father had often used to train him... But it sure felt like one.

Slappy rounded the back, opened the trailer, and pointed in. "Go on."

Evil followed and looked.

The trailer was plain, bare metal on the inside. Bleachers made from the same metal lined both walls. Six metal loops to secure handcuffs lined each side. Each seat had a lap belt and those shoulder ones that make an *X* across the chest. This was nothing more than a regular non-powered prisoner transport.

In Primazone, the trailer would've had two doors on the side and each would open into separated dampening cells. Even the lowest tier of non-powered citizens would be transported in the cells in case they had powers and were in hiding.

Slappy frowned. "I said, *get in.*"

Evil got in as a nostalgic smile spread his lips.

He had once asked his father why would someone with powers hide them and pretend they didn't have any. For once, his father was stumped. That was one question his power-proud father couldn't answer.

Stepping up and in made the last two years of Evil's life feel like a very pleasant dream. A dream he was being woken up from. A dream of not having powers—at least pretending not to—and having a different, non-demanding lifestyle. In Ultrava, there were always expectations of him to use his powers for the betterment of Primazone and the welfare of his country's citizens.

He had noticed kids in the States "off" during their

Summer Break. Pretending to be Ernest Smith Junior had been Evil's summer break. And now school was back in session.

Evil walked to the back and sat on the hard, unforgiving bench.

While he hadn't been sure before, he now knew that even if he hadn't been able to strike a deal to take over the onus of Ernest Smith Junior's life, he would've still found joy in working at Norwest Grind as a frontline coffee slinger. It had been risky propositioning Ernest, but if the co-owner had said no, Evil would've gotten a new false ident and new falseface from Jimmy Alcazar so he could work in another coffee joint.

Slappy waited for them to have eye contact before slamming the door shut and making a loud production of engaging the lock.

Ignoring Slappy, Evil grinned to himself.

Before he'd left Ultrava, he was being groomed to be the next ruler of Primazone, the most powerful nation on the planet. Now? He chuckled. Now, he was content to grind out a paycheck-to-paycheck life. Of course, none of that would've been possible without partnering with super-genius Jimmy Alcazar, who helped Evil in his small crime of working a job before America's legal age.

Evil's mother used to say that she wanted him happy. Not to be a dictator or to be beholden to his lineage. To be able to be present in his own life. Just present and happy. And he had been until the Power League's black ops team had taken the simple life from him. Did any of them stop to think why someone—who could have anything they wanted in the world—would choose to work in a coffee shop?

Evil tried not to think like his father and start plotting ways to make them pay, to retaliate against them, to teach them to leave a sleeping giant be.

The trailer lurched into action and began to arc back the way it came.

Through the turn, Evil's bemused grin faded.

His jaw tightened and his lips curled to mirror the disdainful sneer that typically crawled onto his father's face whenever the man looked at the world and thought about the mass of non-powered beyond their boarders.

Evil's father had taken his mother's life and the League had stolen Evil's happiness, his mother's sole inheritance to him. Though his great-grandfather had seized his father, the League was still out there and doing this to who knows how many other people with powers who'd rather just lay low.

He paused to check his thoughts. Was that last bit presumptuous? Were there so many other hidden, powered people out there that the League had to form a black ops team to handle the super quiet minority?

A hard bump popped Evil from the bench. He came back down on his tailbone. The impact reported up his spine. The metal knobs on the vest truly worked.

Smarting from one of the downsides to not having armored skin and fortified innards, Evil pulled his seatbelts and clicked them in place. Snug against the metal bench, he went back to his thoughts.

If it was just being presumptuous, and all this had been done just for him, what was the purpose? His father had already delivered on his highly televised threat when Evil's mom hadn't returned them to Ultrava by the end of that first week. So, why would the Power League still be after him? The worst thing he had done in America was underage working and possession of someone else's ident.

No. This had to be bigger than just him.

Again, Evil's mind turned to go along the vengeance route that his father had instilled early and reinforced through the years. His mother would've hope for better from him, but someone had to pay.

Evil narrowed his eyes. Someone was going to pay.

Chapter Five

NEW FISH

THE CRUNCH from the rocky dirt under the convoy's tires had given way to a steady droning hum of rolling on well-tended roads. Though fuming, the constant soothing sound had lulled Evil to sleep.

EVIL ROCKED TO A HARD STOP.

He woke still in the back of the trailer and still belted to the bench.

From outside, a male voice droned, "Code?"

The driver, the same guy who mocked a Norwest Grind order, answered, "Tango fourteen fifty-seven union."

The bored guy stated, "Confirmed, tango fourteen." He then asked, "Another beer run?"

The driver started to say something, but Slappy spoke over him. "Whiskey foxtrot golf hotel."

"Golf hotel?" Excitement took hold of the formerly bored guy. "Copy that! Will relay." The sound of metal rattling and scraping came from outside. "Clear to roll, tango fourteen! You know where to go."

The ever so quiet whine of acceleration accompanied their forward movement. Not moving at the same speed as before, there were a series of turns broken up by five to twenty seconds of straightaway.

Evil's father's training took over and he tracked the turns in his mind to get a sense of the layout. They hadn't done enough lefts or rights to head back toward the entry point, so this wasn't a maze to confuse passengers. No, it was just a huge complex with plenty of places where either checkpoints, choke points, or kill points could've been set up.

After a fifty-second straightaway, the Humvee slowed and stopped.

The Humvee rocked slightly both directions as the driver door was closed and the passenger door was slammed. Other car doors sounded around the front of the Humvee. Hurried footsteps laced into a series of clacks, like rifles and handguns being cocked, circling outside as inaudible—almost indistinct—telepathic buzz flashed through the air.

Anyone without telepathy wouldn't have noticed the private missive, but Evil did. If he didn't still have the chunks of metal on his inhibitor vest, he might've been able to hear what had just been said.

With less fanfare than it was engaged, the lock on the trailer was undone and the doors opened.

Sunlight poured in.

Evil squinted.

Slappy said, "Come on out."

Evil unclicked his seatbelts, placed his thumbs on the vest's release latches, and walked to the door. He paused there to give his eyes time to adjust. There was a musty gym-bag smell to the air.

Before now, there had only been men in black with weapons pointed at him. Those same men were present, but their numbers were doubled by men and women in full-body desert camo bodysuits. Bodysuits that were fashioned after the Power League's full body spandex-like titanium mesh suits. Only these were much thicker. Either first gen armor or a new style beefed up for even better protection.

They used all black out in the field, but desert camo inside? The camo print on their domed goggles was just too much camo. It almost felt like he was captive to a joint colony between black ants and camo ants.

Even though Evil was trying to remain stoic, that thought, and the absurdity of the two teams wearing possibly each other's uniforms, forced a smirk to his mouth. It was either that, or whoever set up these uniforms had their wires crossed.

The entire area was un-striped smooth asphalt. The forty or so gunmen formed a firing arc forty feet away from the trailer. No chance for them firing into each other.

The asphalt stretched out beyond them three hundred feet to black, long, five-story-tall buildings. The sunlight lay dull on the surface in a manner unlike anything Evil had seen before. Glass would shine, metal would reflect, and the seams in brickwork would repel the sunshine differently than the bricks themselves.

There was none of that. Just an unnatural absorbing-like effect.

Each corner of those building had far-reaching antenna that were also made of—or covered with—the same sun-soaking black material that jutted into the blue sky. The cloud cover had thinned way out and there wasn't a hill or mountain to be seen.

Slappy ordered, "Step out."

Evil hopped down and instantly remember how sore his feet had gotten.

"The parade is that way." Slappy pointed off to Evil's right where more black buildings with black antenna stood nearly a thousand feet away.

They could've parked closer. Much closer. There had to be a reason for the long walk, but what was it?

Mumbling, "Parade indeed." Evil started walking.

The firing arc matched his pace in a smooth sideways marching movement to keep from getting in each other's way and to constantly remain on Evil's left.

Perhaps that was the reason. So they could show off just how organized they were with their marching band synchronicity.

"New fish!"

Evil's head snapped right to find the voice.

Between the dozen of haphazardly parked Humvees, instead of more buildings three hundred feet away, there were about fifty guys in bright yellow prison-like jumpsuits. Black metal collars obscured part of their necks.

Though there were no walls or marks on the asphalt to indicate where to go or not go, the group of them stayed in the same six-hundred-foot-square rec area that had two basketball courts, a spattering of tennis courts, a handball court, a volleyball court, and on the far side, a quarter-sized American football field.

Looking them over, the world dimmed ever so slightly for a split second; three of the men in yellow stood out: an emaciated man covered in brown fur, a portly African, and a spindly bald white guy. All three weren't interacting with anyone else and they had their backs to Evil.

He glanced up. No heavy clouds nearby. His TA had powered through the nullifiers for a moment to light the most dangerous inmates.

Evil's guts tightened as he could see almost all the prisoners in yellow—all guys, probably two hundred strong—eventually turned to look his way. They all looked like the type of strongmen that get hired on for jobs and left behind for not keeping up. Nothing about this made him think he would see a happy-go-lucky person over there, but each one of them—except for the three—was sizing him up.

While nowhere near as hostile, he'd gotten this same kind of vibe when he had walked onto the schoolyard exclusively for the children of high-tiered ultrahumans in Ultrava. Some of those kids had tried to see if they were more powerful or faster than he was to set the pecking order.

Evil had made his father proud that day by showing off his dominance, but those were kids in a controlled environment owned by his family. And this wouldn't be like training with the Prime Guard. If he bested any of these men, they wouldn't congratulate him. No, they would probably form a gang to beat him down.

A catcall whistle ripped the air when he passed the end of the Humvees.

Separated by a hundred feet was a second six-hundred-foot, equally equipped, area. There were four women in there. Yellow jumpsuits. Black collars. Three were huddled close together near the center of the area. They continued talking while glancing his way. One—short, muscular, with an extra set of arms just above her hips—stood at the nearest corner. She waved at him with her upper right arm.

Another whistle. It was the four-armed woman. She slinked along an invisible line to the rec area at the same pace he was walking. She'd wink at him and blow an occasional kiss.

Evil didn't notice the fifth woman in there until Four-Arms did a nimble sideways flip over her at the halfway mark.

This fifth one sat cross-legged and watched him passively. The way she sat—back straight, palms resting precisely in the middle of her upper legs, thumbs over the top, with her elbows tucked to her sides—was exactly how he was taught to sit patiently in kindergarten. In fact, the only way he didn't sit that way when sitting on the floor was if he purposefully thought against it.

Who was she?

Evil studied her slim face. Her rounded cheeks, chin, and skin tone made her every bit of the stereotypical Hispanic woman he'd come across in Ultrava. However, something about her eyes being full open instead of resting at three-quarter or half-lidded signaled that she somehow recognized him, even with the falseface on.

What did she see?

Was it how he was walking? There hadn't been anything else to go on. Besides Slappy, none of the guards had said a word.

Slappy said, "Keep walkin'."

Evil hadn't noticed he had slowed. He picked up his pace.

"That's right." Slappy hadn't change position or relative distance since the back of the truck. "Don't get any ideas."

Evil adopted the sitting woman's passive expression as he turned dull eyes upon Slappy's sunglasses.

Given that he hadn't had any sort of *ideas*, Evil presumed Slappy didn't have telepathy and was just clueing in on his expressions and body language. Besides, Evil knew the nuanced feeling well and it didn't feel like someone was in the part of his brain where surface thoughts swam.

Slappy nodded at him. "Just keep on walkin'."

Though Four-Arms whistled for his attention, Evil didn't turn to look at the prisoners. If he were to look back, it would be to try and figure out who cross-legged woman was and that didn't seem to be a good idea. Rather it would get her Four-Arms' wrath or scrutiny if Slappy and the others picked up on his interest in her.

Instead he let his gaze range the black antennas on the uniform black buildings, trying to discern the layout and patterns to the buildings beyond the front row. While this wasn't like any televised version of an American prison that Evil had seen, he began to evaluate if being in one was better than being back with his great-grandfather.

Yes. Yes, it was.

Hands down.

Evil barely finished the thought before the answer sprang to his mind. No need for lists or comparisons. It just was. Even this walk with Slappy and Co. was nothing compared to how tightly he would be watched, controlled, and tested in Ultrava.

Slappy said, "I said, *don't get any ideas*."

The firing squad arc stopped moving.

Evil did too and nodded to his thoughts. A physical prison was better than the invisible one in Ultrava, but being free bested both of them. He hadn't done anything to forfeit his freedom in America and so he set his mind to getting it back.

Chapter Six

TWO TYPES OF PRISONERS

THE FIRING SQUAD had rotated to his left a bit and stomped as they came to a stop. Weapons aimed down, they stood at a modified parade rest.

Evil stopped and faced them. However, his brain continued moving on about enduring this prison complex and its gym-bag smell for only as long as necessary.

Slappy pointed the way they'd been walking. "I didn't say to stop. Keep goin'."

Keeping his ears perked for any indication that the squad had taken aim at him again, Evil turned and took a slow step forward.

There were two men without masks in black tac gear outside of the black building. He recognized John Bunyan instantly. The twelve-foot-tall ultrahuman and ex-Canadian Mountie was hard to miss. There were videos of him growing in size up to fifty feet tall. There was also video of him being slain by Srats, a Canadian-born villain with the power to shift into gaseous states. A power he used to penetrate into the lungs of anyone not doing as he willed, and he could turn to a myriad of poisonous gases.

Though Evil's mom had closed the laptop from the live news stream, he had watched it later. The vision of the massive Bunyan panicked, pained, and grasping at his thick neck had stayed with Evil for nearly a month. Blood poured from his eyes, mouth, and ears. It had been the most blood Evil had seen since his father's last torturing of a foreign spy. Just like the spy, John Bunyan in the video had no way of stopping was what happening to him. And, like the spy, the news the next day reported that Bunyan was dead.

Yet, here he was. Looking strong, every bit the opposite of dead. Wait. If Bunyan was a part of the staff, were they in Canada? Canada was supposed to be snowy and cold, but the temperature felt fine, and there hadn't been any sign of snow.

The unassuming, blond crew cut man with blue eyes next to Bunyan cleared his throat and spoke with a drill instructor's cadence. "We call this place Nowhere. It's where the world sends ultrahumans it cannot handle." He motioned openhanded to the holding areas. "Some have escaped prisons in the past. Some are too deadly to be with other prisoners. Hell, some—like yourself—have never seen the inside of a courtroom. However, here they are—like you—in Nowhere." He crossed his arms as he finished.

The man had a high, slightly turned in set to his shoulders. For his outside appearance and way of speaking, he didn't have the bearing of a military man; he didn't have the steel of a soldier.

"In Nowhere," the man continued, "we have outside prisoners and inside prisoners. We start everyone off as insiders. Misbehave and you become an outsider." He afforded himself a smile. "The rules for outsiders are rather..." The man trailed off as though he had to find a word.

Evil was sure he knew the word. This was the man's welcoming speech. Of course he knew the word.

"Minimal." The man's smile faded and his blue eyes

emptied out. "The rules are minimal because it matches our care. I am not going to risk the lives of my good people to stop a beef being settled. So, if a fight breaks out, it breaks out." He shrugged his high shoulders. "And if someone's killed, they're killed." He sucked his teeth. "One less asshole in the world."

Bunyan gave an approving grunt.

"After the fight, or after the murder, we conduct an investigation. If the murderer was in the right, they continue on. And if not—" he motioned his head to the guards at parade rest, "—we put them down." He sucked his teeth again as he shrugged. "One less asshole in the world."

Evil winced. Something about the high shoulders, empty blue eyes, and teeth sucking pulled at memories in his head.

Memories that weren't his.

They, the two of them, were in their usual cozy candlelit private dining room at Casa di Ricordi. The Lovers' Waltz *played softy from obscured speakers. The heady perfume from the two dozen long-stem roses in the tall crystal vase on a stand next to their small table was intoxicating.*

All that, along with the masterful Italian food and perfectly paired wine created a floating sensation.

This night was a very special celebration. They had done this every year for the past twenty years—

Evil snapped out of it. That extreme marker—*twenty years*—was his exit from the memory. In a little over five years, he'd be able to celebrate twenty years of being alive; twenty years of anything else would have to come after that.

While almost always a boon, sometimes other people's power-memories overtaking his senses were a drawback.

Rarely, like now, it was a matter of timing. Usually, though, the memory flash was of an intense moment in the person's life that always related to the stolen power. His father had advised him to ride each memory wave to its completion because the key to what all the power in question could do lay within the memory. The memory could have a major power stunt or a subtle, nuanced trick. The flashes were always grab bags and the only way to know was to hang in there and hope that one recollection rolled into another.

Evil had lost sync with what was being said.

The blond hadn't lost steam. "Your one goal in your life from here on out, or what should be your goal, is to not become an outsider." He pivoted sideways.

Bunyan did the same and took a step back.

The blond extended his hand, opened palm to the building. "So, all that said, I invite you inside for processing."

A suction sound, like a top coming off of a jar, came from the building. A thin, eight-foot-tall, vertical white line of light appeared in the black façade. As the line widened, the light decreased to reveal a dull white room ten feet across and deep. The three walls in there were bare, devoid of decoration, windows, or doors.

Something about the room felt like a trap. Then again, the trap-business had already happened and been taken care in the alley behind Norwest Grind. Since he was already caught and still in custody, they didn't have to re-capture him.

Yet, something felt *off* about the room. Evil couldn't say what exactly, but he felt it deep down and he'd come to trust those feelings.

Evil took a deep breath and said, "No, thank you."

"What?" The blond frowned. "Did you just decline my hospitality?"

Evil nodded.

The blond scratched his temple as the right corner of his

mouth twisted up in confusion. “So, you’re choosing to be an outsider?”

Evil answered, “*Indeed, Pauly.*” He had meant to say *yes*. Where the heck did *indeed, Pauly* come from? Why had he said that and why did he say it with such a you’re-not-the-boss-of-me attitude.

The blond stumbled back as though Evil had battered him with a psionic attack.

“Boss?” Bunyan started toward the man before stopping himself. He glared at Evil and grew minutely as all the muscles in his body tensed. In the blink of an eye, Bunyan hoisted one of his massive fists back.

Evil dodged backward. Wind whiffed past him as Bunyan missed.

Bunyan’s follow-up punch was right behind the first.

Evil bobbed. He didn’t want to be there when the second punch came in. However, without an ounce of his enhanced prowess, *want* was all he had as the world flashed bright blue from Bunyan’s knuckles impacting with the vest’s pinpoint forcefield and the forcefield popped liked a blown lightbulb.

Guards gasped.

Though the brunt of Bunyan’s punch was absorbed, there was still steam on the second swing and Bunyan’s big fist hit the right side of Evil’s head, sending him stumbling to keep his feet beneath him.

“Stop, John.” Pauly—the blond—had recovered. “I’m good.”

Legs wobbling, Evil kept at his awkward sideways rush to not fall. He’d been punched many times in his life. Usually harder. But the sensation of the entire side of his head being hit all at once had an unprecedented dizzying effect. It was like both the neck-whipping results from getting punched in the jaw and the you-are-going-sideways feeling from being punched on the temple couldn’t decide which would win the pain race so they held hands as they crossed the finish line.

Evil swooned when he caught his balance.

He was upright-ish. Knees week. His shaky legs felt like rubber. But he was standing. Vision blurred, he focused on the largest distortion that he figured was Bunyan. From habit, he raised his fist to commit to the fight.

The inmates cheered, hooted, and bellowed a cacophony of encouragement.

The vest vibrated like it had the first time Jimmy turned it on. The force of Bunyan's punch must've made it power down. But it was fully back in action even if Evil wasn't.

Pauly yelled through the cheers. "Take the hem out, John."

Concussed, that's what Evil thought he heard. Though the world wasn't making complete sense, he knew what, who, the large advancing blur was and prepared to go with the next shot instead of trying to dodge it.

The right side the blur came closer.

Evil leaned to go with the force.

The world flashed bright blue as the forcefield popped again. The entire left side of Evil's head lit with pain as he stumbled right.

Instinct took over and he struggled to keep his feet beneath him.

In the middle of his realization that this wasn't going to stop until he was unconscious, Evil's plan of going with it snapped back to him and he crumpled—on purpose.

Chapter Seven

AMPED UP

For his eleventh birthday, Evil's father took him to Las Vegas, the city at the northernmost tip of the Primazone, to watch regular humans fight each other in a mixed martial arts tournament. While not initially interested in seeing ***duds duke it out***—as his father would say—Evil began to realize why they had made the trip.

There was something very primal about people without powers fighting one another. No energy blasts, no flying, no high-speed chases. Just two combatants facing each other down in an enclosed and unobstructed area. At the heart of the tournament, it was about who was better and that was only decided by who was not rendered unconscious.

While dazed and probably concussed, Evil was not unconscious. However, in hoping to appear so, he kept his gaze unfocused and didn't attempt to get to his feet or move. Moving might bring in another punch.

A lone gunshot instantly halved cheers from the inmates and they quieted from there.

The asphalt was warm beneath Evil and smelled like it

had only be laid a few months ago. The sky above was so blue and vast. A part of him missed flying.

In America, it was bad form to hit someone when they were down, but Evil wasn't sure they were in America anymore. And, even if they were in the States, this facility was so far outside the realm of what he'd come to know as *normal* in America that it probably would happen anyway.

However, the world over—anger issues and excessive shit talkers aside—unless the plan was to kill the unconscious opponent, it was universally unacceptable to keep pounding on someone who you had clearly rendered unconscious. Some of the most infamous villains did it to heroes, but that fell under the kill the opponent clause.

Two blurry forms, one much larger than the other, leaned over him.

Evil tried to make sense of the clause that he just made up. His mother had pointed out that there were certain unspoken social contracts, like don't drive into oncoming traffic. Evil was sure none of them had a ***kill the opponent*** clause. The Primazone had a clear, never written, ***don't betray the state*** rule, but then again, treason was punishable everywhere.

The big blur, Bunyan, asked, "Should I hit him again?"

Pauly, the small one, said, "Nah. His eyes are open, but he's out. Let's get him into the outsider's intake."

Bunyan scooped Evil from the ground.

Being lifted by Bunyan felt like being picked up by his parents when he was a little kid. However, instead of being wrapped up in a warm hug or hoisted up to see—like taking a stiff medicine ball to the gut, Evil was flopped over Bunyan's wide rock-hard shoulder.

In the process, the metal stubs on his chest were knocked off and thunked on the ground. Instantly, his head cleared.

His tactical awareness came back and assured him that he had made the right move.

"Now! Now! Now!" A woman yelled from the prison area. "Get some!"

Evil felt spurred. Her words dug into him, grabbed him by the soul, and shook him. His adrenaline surged and his blood pumped hard. Body pulsing, his TA got amped up and he was ready to fight.

Thrumming from the amazing physiological surge, Evil managed to keep himself in check.

He could fight his way out, but fighting to get out and staying free were two different things. Unless he could be totally victorious here, leaving no guard conscious—in case they had powers—and destroying all the vehicles, they'd be able to follow him long enough to relay his location and trajectory to the Power League's new black ops team.

And then what?

Fight all of them at once like his great-grandfather had? A battle like that would surely be a blip on Primazone's precogs' radar, and he'd be back under his great-grandfather's yoke.

Still, the surge made him feel...*alive.*

Alive like when Evil's father took him to their remote base in the heart of Antarctica and let him really cut loose on the glaciers. Blasting them. Pounding them. Heaving huge chunks larger than himself.

Even better, he didn't have that post-exertion drain that he'd felt while watching the base's team of cryokinetics repair what he'd done. His father said the lesson that day was to understand that there's always a cleanup and recovery phase after unloading, but unloading was all that Evil truly remembered.

Evil shoved himself from Bunyan's shoulder.

The big man grabbed for him.

Evil dodged. His TA warned of three threats that, according to his TA, would overpower him.

The first was a tall male guard in black who had icy slush circling his right hand.

The second was another male guard, shorter, in black who made huge mustard-yellow hands with mental energy.

Evil bet it was telekinesis.

The third was a female guard in the desert camo. Evil's TA warned him as she had pulled a pistol, pointed at him, and pulled the trigger.

He dodged. His better senses came back to him and he threw his hands up. "Just kidding!" He laced his fingers behind his head and dropped to his knees. "Just kidding."

Bunyan pressed the metal nubs onto Evil's side.

While Evil's head remained clear, his TA went dormant again. Assigning them nicknames, he glanced to Icee, Mustard, and Psygun.

Bunyan pounded him.

Evil's clear head went fuzzy again and he pretended to go limp.

Bunyan flopped Evil back onto his shoulder.

Whatever that woman's surging power was, it was truly impressive. Evil had never experienced anything like it before and—aside from the compulsion to take action—he sort of wanted to feel it again. More than the adrenaline hit, he wanted to feel that rousing in his soul.

The afterglow of the woman's power began to fade.

His focus fully his again, Evil turned his mind back to when he'd escape. It'd have to be low-key. Better yet, entirely unnoticed to give him plenty of time to fly to a big city and get lost in the crowds.

For now, though, he was along for the ride as Bunyan steadily walked them toward intake.

Chapter Eight

FACE OFF

THAT JAR OPENING suction sound that accompanied the building opening hit the air. Unable to see the way they were going, Evil watched the ground. The asphalt ended at a thin line of black metal where white tile flooring began.

Not far in, Bunyan took Evil off his shoulder and set him down.

Icee, Mustard, and Psygun passed him and went further into the room.

The floor looked like tile, but had a stiff sponginess like a new gym mat. Like the other white room, this one was right off the asphalt, too, a fifteen-foot cube. Each of the three walls were one long smooth dull white laminate. From floor to ceiling, tiny pinprick-sized holes dotted the wall. They were a foot apart from each other and made the room look, and feel, like a gas chamber. Identical, the ceiling offered nothing new, not even lights.

Since the walls opened directly to the outside, it made sense that the air was similar. However, in the room, there was a slight fruity—strawberry—scent.

The white exterior closed from both sides like dual sliding

glass doors to meet in the middle. When they made contact, the white from both sides drew together to obscure the seam with the uniform laminate look and gave off light as though the sun still came through; which it didn't. The foot-apart pinpricks from the floor to the ceiling were the only marks showing where the split had been. But that line of floor to ceiling dots looked exactly like the lines of dots a foot to its right and left.

Was the whole place modular?

Further in the room, Pauly said, "You cannot see out, but they can see in. Typically, it's the other way around."

Still amazed by the wall and what the various dots implied, Evil asked, "So, can this wall, these walls, open on the dots?"

"Doesn't matter." There was a tension in Pauly's voice that wasn't there before. He said, "You chose to be an outsider. That decision forfeited your right to question anything about this building. Now, take off your falseface."

Evil turned.

Bunyan stood with his arms crossed behind Pauly, who also had his arms crossed. Both men looked stern, but anger rimmed Pauly's eyes and tight jaw.

Icee, Mustard, and Psygun were behind them.

Evil placed his index fingers behind his ears and waited for the faint bell that acknowledged his fingerprints. Thin fasteners popped from behind his ears and the occoflect material around his head and neck relaxed. He shuddered as the mask's anchor points in his ears and nostrils released and fell loose. That always felt weird. The anchor points just inside his mouth and around his eyes let go next.

Not quiet enough, Bunyan whispered, "That's some new FF tech there, Boss. I've never seen nothing like it."

All loose, Evil grabbed his Ernest mask by the nose and pulled it off.

Bunyan stiffened. "You're a kid." He looked down at Pauly. "He's a kid."

Pauly's narrowed eyes widened slightly.

Evil corrected, "I'm a teen."

"What?" Incredulous, Bunyan asked, "Thir*teen?*"

Evil glared at the big man. "I'm *four*teen."

"Bullshit." Pauly scoffed. "You think you're so clever." He pointed at Evil's face. "Take off that second falseface."

"Can't." Evil shrugged. "Because there isn't one."

Pauly closed on him.

Evil stood his ground.

Pauly got in Evil's face. His blue eyes making a study of the typical spots where lesions would form from overuse of normal falsefaces. Pauly then stepped to Evil's right to inspect his profile, looking for the almost imperceptible change that all falsefaces had over the eyes and eyelashes.

Pauly yanked the occoflect material from Evil's hand and gawked at Ernest's features still being present on the unwrapped mask.

Jimmy's improvement on falsefaces had taken Evil aback, too. Since Evil wanted to imitate one person in particular, Jimmy made his tech specific. So, instead of having a mask that was programmable to look like the person the wearer wanted to imitate, Jimmy imprinted the cloth with Ernest's likeness. That feature alone had bypassed the few falseface ident scans that Evil had stumbled across.

Bunyan said, "Boss, the other side."

Pauly flipped it over. "Who's this?"

"Me." Evil answered.

Icee, Mustard, and Psygun exchanged glances with one another.

Pauly sneered at the mask. "You?"

"Yeah." Evil nodded at his age-progressed features with

Danny Trejo's skin complexion as it was close to his own skin tone before he started absorbing powers.

Evil continued, "Just with—" and stopped. He was about to volunteer information to men who would only hear the worst in his words or use the info against him. He was going to say *just without darkness*. That's what the upper echelon called the tint that accumulated in the cells of a body from absorbing others' powers. It was a mark of power and potential, and certainly nothing to be ashamed of. These five wouldn't understand.

Pauly put his hands together to drape most of the face over his palms. "Just with a beard."

Evil nodded as he defaulted back to only speaking when silence wouldn't be accepted.

Pauly tucked it into his pants pocket like a trophy bandana. "Why a beard?"

Evil turned his head slightly to look Pauly in the eye. As he noted the twitch in Pauly's right eye, Evil knew that Pauly was going to hit him. He couldn't put his finger on why he knew that. An eye twitch was rather common, but as Pauly balled his fist, Evil presumed the knowledge came from the same source in him that knew that the guy's name was Pauly.

Pauly's eye twitched harder and his arm shook as he spoke through a grimace. "I asked you a question."

"Well." The part of Evil that knew these things about Pauly wanted to remain defiant, but he used this moment to cement his age. "I've found that a mask that makes me look older avoids questions that I get asked without it." Evil flipped his apron. "You know, jobs, apartments, and stuff that teens in America can't do without—" His voice lifted. "*Permission from Papa.*"

Pauly uncorked a rabbit punch into Evil's gut.

Made to handle much tougher assaults, the vest's forcefield barely lit as it absorbed the impact.

Evil winced. Not from any physical discomfort, but confusion. That was twice today where a close alternate to what he wanted to say came out of his mouth instead of exactly what he wanted to say. While he hadn't had time to think about the first one, the you're-not-the-boss-of-me feeling coupled with the deep desire to be defiant signaled a clash of consciousnesses. Someone Evil had absorbed was close to Pauly. Knew him well and developed a lot of their power-knacks as a directly result of Pauly.

His father had fully explained this downside of absorption. It was exactly the reason why you were supposed to focus solely on the person's powers, rejecting everything else, when syphoning. The less you knew of the person, the less likely this was to happen. Evil had seen it close to a dozen times with his father and once with his great-grandfather, but today was his first. And second.

Pauly pointed in Evil's face. "Watch your mouth."

Evil tightened his lips and jaw as more words tried to make their way out. Closed mouth, the mumble had a ton of attitude and the words were clear in his head. *Or what? You're going to beat me like you did your wife?*

Pauly's voice became a harsh whisper. "What did you just say?"

"Or what." Evil lied, "You're going to put me outside?" And was thrilled that he said what he meant to say.

Pauly put his whole body behind the next rabbit punch.

The forcefield shone a little brighter as it absorbed the impact.

Evil doubled over a bit and stumbled back. That was the reaction that Pauly wanted and if he didn't get it, he'd keep increasing the force.

"Paul, stop!" Bunyan got between them. "He's a kid."

Icee, Mustard, and Psygun were also shaken, but they stayed where they were.

Pauly went to get around Bunyan. "The little shit is goading me."

"Even so." Bunyan blocked Pauly with ease. "He's still a kid. A minor. I don't know if we can even keep him here."

"We can." Pauly stepped back from Bunyan, trying to compose himself. "We will. We have to."

Bunyan tried to whisper, but clearly his lungs weren't used to easing air out. "There's other facilities for cases like this. Like him."

"No, this is uncharted." Pauly whispered true whispers. He then raised his voice. "Besides, even with the nullifier on, he could take a punch from you and dig in my head to push buttons that—" Almost teary, Pauly's voice faltered.

He tried to pass Bunyan.

With a step, the big man blocked him.

Evil took note of just how quick on his feet Bunyan could be. The guy had the prowess to match most combat focused ultrahumans.

Pauly stopped and walked backward. His eyes were bloodshot. Obviously not wanting to be seen as weak, he turned away from Evil. And instantly turned back around to keep from facing the prisoners who probably looked on with great interest.

Pauly said, "Door."

The suction sound came and Evil watched the wall leading farther in to the black building complex part like elegant traditional Japanese sliding doors. Beyond the wall was a white hallway just like the room that ran parallel with the wall.

Bunyan kept himself between them as Pauly walked around Evil.

Pauly stopped by the three ultrahuman guards and said, "Get him in a jumpsuit."

"But he's a kid," Bunyan replied and wrung his hands. "We can't put him out there with them."

Pauly spun. "Ext-wall. Opaque."

The natural light was snuffed out and replaced by wall and ceiling lighting like massive LED bulbs.

Pauly pointed at Evil. "That *kid* is the most powerful ultrahuman that we've had. Even the inhibitor nubs cannot take away all of his power. Put a collar on him, get him in a jumpsuit, and put him out there."

Bunyan was shaking his head.

"Man up." Pauly yanked the falseface from his pocket. "Have him wear this beard out. If they mess with him, he'll be able to defend himself." He tossed the occoflect cloth as Bunyan.

Bunyan caught it. "But—"

"But nothing." Paul bared his teeth. "He is the descendant of Supreme Overlord. He knows how to handle salty ultrahumans." Pauly walked between the three guards, out of the room, and said, "Close."

The wall slid closed.

Bunyan looked at the face on the cloth in his hand and then to Evil. "Well." Leaning his head to the side, his neck cracked several loud, rapid pops. "I would prefer to do this the easy way."

Chapter Nine

PROCESSING

WITH PAULY GONE, the defiance simmering deep in Evil faded.

Just before Evil's mother talked him into going with her to America, he had squared off with his father over how Evil was running his city. His father wanted him to order his Peacekeepers to sweep the city for a suspected spy. Evil and his lieutenants had already uncovered and identified the spy and were watching him to discover the spy network—if there was one.

But Evil didn't tell his father that. It was his city and he was taking care of it. His father had warned him against defying him. Evil had known the definition of the word, but hadn't felt it until after. After his father insisted, after they fought, and after Evil lost. Upon being told the scope of what Evil had his Peacekeepers doing, Evil's father had been proud of him, but—beaten badly—Evil found no joy in his father's praise, only more defiance.

Evil took, and exhaled, a deep breath. The strawberry scent had overtaken the outside smell just like the here and now overtook both wants for defiance.

He nodded to Bunyan and said, "More with honey than vinegar."

"Yup." Bunyan gave his own sigh of relief.

Though they were quiet, the two guys in black and the woman in camo stayed at the ready.

"Collar." Bunyan reached his hand up to the ceiling. A small hatch slid open. A black metal collar, like the ones the Evil saw on the prisoners outside, fell into the big man's hand. The hatch slid close.

Bunyan added, "And a jumpsuit for non-staff."

The light from the walls intensified for a moment and faded. A bong sounded from the upper four corners. "Anomaly noted."

Surprised to hear a voice he knew so well, Evil glanced at the corners for a camera and asked, "Jimmy?" There still were no visible cameras.

The bong sounded from the upper four corners and Jimmy said, "Voice prompt denied. User's voice not authorized to issue commands." Though it was Jimmy's voice, there was an inflectionless, atonal quality to it.

Icee, Mustard, and Psygun tightened up and looked at Bunyan, who had done the same.

Suspicion laced Bunyan's words when he asked, "How do you know Jimmy?"

Without hesitation, Evil replied, "In the Primazone, we make it our business to know world shapers." Evil never thought he would have to use that line, but—in exchange for his help—Jimmy had asked Evil to repeat it a hundred times and he had. Because it meant a lot to Jimmy, Evil had even made it part of his morning mantra-thoughts. Repeating it now was as easy as breathing. It rolled off his tongue.

Seemingly at a loss, Bunyan asked, "Who are the other world shapers?"

Evil hadn't thought it would go this way, but Jimmy had

been right. The person questioning him, Bunyan in this case, focused on the last of the sentence.

Jimmy had said the sentence was clever social engineering because no one really knew what happened behind the scenes in his great-grandfather's country so they would focus on who else his great-grandfather was keeping an eye on, thus normalizing how Evil knew Jimmy. Or, in this case, his voice.

Evil shook his head as another automatic reply came from his mouth. "National security. Sorry."

His father had told him that should be his reply to his mother for any—and every—time she asked about what he, his father, or his great-grandfather did or felt. No matter how minor. An automatic reply that his mother had challenged the first day they were in America and she asked how he liked his burger.

He didn't know if his great-grandfather really had a watch list, but it was a clever diversion.

Bunyan asked, "Jimmy, what's the anomaly?"

Jimmy's atonal voice replied, "The x-ray scan of the unknown body in the room has revealed an abnormal layer of clothing."

A black outline of Evil's body, exact height, how he was standing and all, dimmed on each wall. On the black, a black-rimmed white outline denoted the shape and contours of his apron, long sleeve polo, pants, and vans lit. They then flew away from the black outline like a blowout of a diagrammed engine. It blurred Evil's genitals, but the white vest remained on his black outline.

Bunyan motioned to the vest on the silhouette. "Take it off."

Evil didn't comply.

The main reason he bought the vest from Jimmy was to dial down his mental signature so that the telepaths couldn't get a lock on him. If he took it off, he would light up and they would get a fix on his location. Once that happened, his great-grandfather would be here in an instant to take him home, and probably destroy the prison and kill everyone in sight just because that's where Evil was being hidden.

He extended his hand. "Inhibitor collar first."

"What?" Bunyan appeared to be at a loss but got back on point. "I said take it off."

Evil shrugged, "What's so wrong with me wanting to put the collar on first?"

Bunyan's face screwed up in concentration. "The fact that you want to put it on."

Evil's eyes rolled. "It's not a Br'er Rabbit, briar patch trick. This vest *is* an inhibitor. I bought it and wear it to hide from telepaths. If I take the vest off, I'm going to light up the mental realm and then the hell that is my great-grandfather will demolish your precious little prison."

While the three behind Bunyan shifted uncomfortably, the big man looked unconvinced.

Evil said, "Look. Just as most people here don't want to die, I don't want to go back to Primazone. It's a long story that I'm not going to share. Wherever he finds me, he's going to do worse than he did in Barstow. That was to prove a point to not defy him. What do you think he'll do if he thinks—which he will—that everyone here kept me, the only heir, from him?"

Bunyan remained skeptical.

Icee, Mustard, and Psygun glances.

Psygun cleared her throat and said, "John, it might sound like a trick, but what harm can come from him putting the collar on first?"

Bunyan said, "He's already shown that he has tech beyond ours. For all we know, that vest could somehow interact with the collar to turn off the prisoners' collars. Instant riot."

Evil found a level of respect for Bunyan. He had the right

amount of paranoia, as what he said was exactly the type of far-reaching plans that Evil's father loved to talk about. A fond smile turned his lips. Intricate planning was the one activity that almost always put his father in a good mood. Being the only way that Evil could manipulate his father, Evil had started making his own plans by the age of three and had truly awed his father with one when he was eight. From then on, Evil's father included him in all of the daily planning sessions, not just the nightly *what ifs* before bed.

He wanted to congratulate Bunyan and share how many contingency plans he had made for escape—albeit from his great-grandfather's Peacekeepers if they came after him—in his daily life to validate the man's fear, but didn't. Those plans remained good if Evil ever went back to the neighborhood, and the hyperloop he had built under G14 was a legitimate escape tunnel or access point.

Evil touched his lips in disbelief at the swell of affection for his father. A man he clearly still admired and despised.

Bunyan noticed that action and it made his other hand ball into a fist. "You haven't taken it off."

Using the expression, Evil pretended as though mirth had bubbled up from within. He laughed.

Bunyan bristled.

The three behind Bunyan exchanged glances again. Psygun looked purposefully at Icee and motioned her head toward Bunyan in a *you try* type of way.

Icee shook his head.

"Okay." Evil said, "Before I do it your way, let me see if I get the big picture that you're concerned about." He brought his facial expression back into his normal range to continue with a straight face. "You think that I am wearing this vest because I planned on being captured and taken to a place where I could short out restraining devices to release whoever happened to be wherever I was taken?"

Bunyan's gazed dipped. "You come from those kinds of thinkers. Look at what you dad did."

"But he had a reason." Evil bit his lip. "Well, he had a reason to him. My mother and me leaving him set him off. Even if he had the plan to make an ethnicity extinct before he was my age, he didn't have a reason to act." Evil raised his hands to the sky, hoping that he could grab some sense and layer it over Bunyan. "What reason would I have to do what you think I *may be* trying to do? Hmm?"

Psygun looked to Mustard and gave him the same *you try* head motion.

Mustard shook his head, too.

Evil pointed to the wall that would lead to the outside. "You think I let myself be captured to free someone out there who is a prisoner in a place that I didn't even know existed?"

Bunyan narrowed his eyes. "Your name is *Evil*. There's no telling what kind of crazy, vile, mastermind stuff is going on in your head."

Evil shuddered. "Fine." He loathed his name and hated being called it. "You want me to take this off?" He put his fingers on the release switch. "You asked for—"

"Damn it, Bunyan!" Psygun blurted. She said, "Just give him the collar."

Bunyan's big face screwed up in a scowled as he looked behind him. "I outrank you."

She nodded. "And you could easily kick my ass, but the possible threat of all those prisoners out there—if you're right—pales in comparison to the possible threat that Supreme Overlord will come if he's right.

Icee said, "Yeah."

Mustard chimed in. "I'd rather take my chances against all of them than against him." The way the guy said *him*, it sounded like the *h* was capitalized in his mind.

Bunyan turned back to Evil. His scowl had deepened.

Evil kept his fingers in place. "In your scenario, I'm a get out of jail card. In my scenario, I'm a doom bringer. In both scenarios, I have a high survival probability." Evil's gazed dipped as guilt crawled up on his shoulders. Even more lives that were going to be lost because of his selfish action of not going back home when his dad had televised his ultimatum.

Even though Bunyan was forcing the situation, Evil's old nagging feeling that he had been right in disagreeing with his mom about having free will came back stronger than before. He'd never get out of his family shadow. He wished that he had never left in the first place. His mother, and her people, would still be alive.

Evil raised his gazed to meet Bunyan's again. "It's your fate." Trying to absolve himself for his part in what was going to happen, he sighed and said, "You make the call."

Chapter Ten

PROPER FEAR OF SUPREME

THE ROOM'S temperature seemed to drop suddenly. While the strawberry smell had grown even stronger, almost sickening, the room's temp was the same. The chill was in Evil's guts. He'd said that he had a high probability of survival, but the quality of his life would change if taken back.

Evil had once seen his great-grandfather exert telepathic possession over Ground Zero—an ultrahuman with the ability to survive detonating his body to destroy a city block—when the assassin had come to kill his great-grandfather's advisors on Ultrava's 50th anniversary.

Though his father had later explained that the identical reddish-purple light that had emitted from both his great-grandfather's and Ground Zero's eyes was mental energy only visible to powerful telepaths, that had been the least unsettling aspect of watching the controlled assassin calmly lift a manhole cover, walk around with it all through the celebration, and—late that night—walk into a swimming pool to lay underneath it. No death throes as the stream of bubbles coming from his mouth to the surface stopped. No last-ditch effort to shirk the control. Just a robot-like acceptance of doing as programmed.

Face screwed in thought, Bunyan was taking longer than anyone else under the threat of death and destruction to choose the *not-death-and-destruction* option. The big man probably thought Evil was bluffing, but this wasn't that kind of game.

If Evil was detected, his great-grandfather would eventually come and unleash the wanton devastation he was infamous for. Death would be swift for the first wave of guards to die, but for the more resolute, there would be suffering until the end. His great-grandfather would accept the word of any of the ultrahuman prisoners who would swear to obey him and destroy the rest, but what would his great-grandfather do with Evil?

Would he be forced to do what Ground Zero did or would his great-grandfather do to Evil what he had done to his own son when Evil's grandfather tried to overthrow his great-grandfather's rule?

The chill in Evil's gut spread through his body. He shuddered.

The night of Ground Zero's forced suicide, Evil's father had told him about how his great-grandfather kept his grandfather in suspended animation and would possess the body to perform raids when the precog core couldn't foresee an unconditionally favorable outcome.

Would Evil also end up in suspended animation next to his grandfather, only to be brought out as a weapon? Would his great-grandfather destroy him like he had Evil's father for the murder of over a billion people? Running away from home paled in comparison to an attempted coup or genocide, but his great-grandfather had a rather stark view of allegiance. And betrayal, no matter how slight, was betrayal.

Reflexively, Evil was already working on a justification for his action. He was deep enough in the thought of survival that he didn't noticed that Bunyan had tossed the hinge-opened black collar to him until the hard metal bopped off his chest.

Bunyan said, "Go ahead. Put it on." He glanced over his shoulder at the woman and men behind him. "If this goes sideways, it's on you guys."

"Thanks." Evil scooped the collar from the ground. It had a little heft to it. He lifted it to his neck and clicked it closed. Too wide at first, the collar whirred and vibrated as it cinched to a tight fit.

"Okay." Bunyan made give-me motions. "Now, the vest."

Evil nodded. "Yup." He took off his apron, peeled off his long sleeve polo, and dropped both on the floor. Whew, it wasn't just his nerves, the room had gone chilly.

Icee asked, "What's up with your hands?"

"Oh." Evil looked at the occoflect gloves that were still the color of Ernest's pale Caucasian skin over his own light brown.

Wow. He hadn't seen his natural skin tone in years. It was a tad lighter than the color he'd had Jimmy make his older self. Evil committed skin tone to memory for if—when—he'd have a chance to change it.

Evil explained, "These are the same material as that." He pointed to his mask. "And they're paired to match skin tones. He slipped the gloves off, dropped them on his polo, and dug his fingers into the latches on his vest.

He paused for a moment and took a deep breath. Not wanting to be a puppet to his great-grandfather or forced to kill himself, Evil hoped that the nullification offered by the collar was enough to keep him below telepathic radar.

Evil pulled the latches. Weighted by the metal nubs that had teleported him, his snug vest went slack and thunked on the floor.

His multitude of powers began to wake as his skin instantly darkened to that gravelly gray color he had been darkening to around his eighth or ninth absorption. While it no longer felt natural to be this color, it was a comfortable middle ground from his natural skin tone and the jet black that overabsorption—if there was truly such a thing—of other ultrahumans' powers turned the skin.

Clearly, the collar did have a nullifying effect but wasn't up to the strength of the vest that, without the metal nubs, dimmed his skin to a milky halftone gray commonly attributed to aliens.

"Anomaly removed." Jimmy's toneless voice said, "Jumpsuit being prepared."

Evil's tactical awareness blossomed, alerting him of the threat level from the four in the room with him and the various weapons on their bodies; oddly, the air also registered as a low-level threat. His empathic reception picked up on Bunyan and crew's growing concern. One of his passive telepathy knacks snagged Bunyan's surface thoughts of this having been a trick, however, his power had not grown strong enough to register mental signatures beyond fifty feet. Enough for an astute telepath to detect a psionic footprint, but below the level of disrupting the psychic landscape.

Evil said, "Well, my great-grandfather didn't show up, so I think we're good."

"Good?" Bunyan pointed at him as the big man's concern started a slow slide toward fear. "You darkened. That isn't good."

Evil countered, "We're still alive." He turned his hand over to study his color. "And what'd you expect? That I'd stay a skin tone that I haven't been since the first grade?"

"Wait." Icee's concern had traveled to the border of confusion. "Your vest had *better* nullification than an Alcazar collar?" His thoughts rippled through a mental link to the others, *Alcazar has the best tech. How is this possible?*

Clearly, Psygun replied. Her mental voice was crisp and dominated the link; she was the telepath. *Whoever he gets his tech from, if he doesn't make it himself, outclasses the folks at Alcazar Industries.*

What do I tell him to do? Bunyan's mental voice had the same cadence, but was a much higher pitch than his physical voice.

That didn't make sense at all. Mental voices of non-telepaths always sound just like their physical voices. Was Bunyan also a telepath? Opening his mouth, Evil almost asked. If Bunyan's telepathy had manifested as a preteen, and he never used it, it'd make sense that his mental voice would still have a prepubescent sound. However, upon discovering the power, almost all telepaths worked to understand it and strengthen it, which is enough to have the mental voice match the physical one.

Evil found his eyes narrowing in suspicion. Something was up there and he couldn't pin it down.

Guys. Psygun was looking at Evil. She tucked her emotions away from casual view and tried to cover the telepath link, but Evil easily read through it. *I don't feel anything from him. He's masking his emotions.*

Mustard shrugged. *Try to read his thoughts.*

"No!" Evil shook his head as Dreamweaver's seeping black eyeballs flashed in his mind's eye. "Don't do that." If what happened to the bounty hunter in the alley happened to her here in the prison, they'd figure it was an attack and Evil probably wouldn't have time to explain that his mind is full of mental traps. Traps laid by one the single most powerful telepaths that Evil had ever known.

"And—" Mustard crossed his arms. "Don't do what, exactly?"

"I don't know," Evil lied. "I sometimes get hunches when things are going to be done to me or I'm about to do something. Those hunches are incredibly strong when whatever is going to be attempted would fail or backfires *and* I get blame."

"You have—" She sighed. "You have *blame sense?*" The woman's voice held enough doubt that it was obvious he had tripped her bullshit meter.

"Well, I wouldn't call it *blame* sense." Evil's mind raced for an explanation to back the weird power he'd just made up. "It's more like *trouble* sense. I felt trouble coming, and since I wasn't going to do anything, I presumed one of you four were going to do something." He had been hoping that he could come up with a story to substantiate the weirdly specific and utterly useless power, but it was so flimsy that it felt like his creativity abandoned him to let him suffer whatever came from that crappy lie.

And they looked entirely ready to jump him, again.

Chapter Eleven

SPINNING A WEB

EVIL'S TA started to lay out the first thirty seconds of combat. Bunyan would come in fast, swinging. Icee and Mustard unleash their powers and Psygun would pull that unique gun that enabled her to shoot psychic bullets.

The best counter move, according to his tactical awareness, was to bust down the wall so the combat could spill outside where there'd be more space and options to work with. It would also get him out of whatever was up with the strawberry air, and—if he played everything just right—possibly free the prisoners to start a riot so that he could fly away in the confusion of the prison guards working to contain the other prisoners.

"The other prisoners." In a play to de-escalate, Evil pointed to the exterior wall. "They're still there, right? Me putting on the nullifier collar wasn't a trick to get them free." He touched it. The inside was warm against his skin, but the outside was cool.

Evil shifted his focus to Bunyan. "I knew that if I did what you wanted and removed my vest first, I would be blamed for what my great-grandfather would've done here."

His creativity engaged and a good lie came to him. "Right now, I'm only wanted for being Supreme's great-grandson, but the world wouldn't know that he'd come here to free me. The last prisoner registered to enter would be me and I would be blamed for every life lost and every vehicle destroyed."

Psygun asked, "So we're back to blame sense?"

"Trouble sense." Evil corrected and then shifted his gaze. "Look. It's a seemingly useless power, but it's strong and has kept me out of trouble this far."

Bunyan grinned. "Well, I just caught you in a lie. You aren't here for your relation to Supreme."

"The hell I'm not." Evil sneered as he tied the obvious incarceration to the deal he had struck with Ernest. "However, I do know that, in three days, I am going to be formally blamed by you people for Ernest Smith's abduction." In thinking on it, Evil prayed Ernest would stick to the plan. He pretended to swoon and recover. "It's going to come out that he'd been missing for three years, a year *before* I came to America. The true kidnappers will remain free to do so again because no one will believe that I, the great-grandson of Supreme, would buy a fake ident and falseface to work in America."

Psygun nodded. "It does sound rather banal." Her stance shifted from being ready to pull her gun with intention to shoot him to just being ready to fight.

"But that's exactly what I was doing." Evil let his true why-the-hell-are-you-folks-even-after-me emotions show. "I was taking out the trash." He stressed, "The trash!" And continued, "When your capture team came to the alley behind Norwest Grind to perform their abduction." It was good that he truly had those feelings as it was illegal to fake emotions in Primazone, so any attempt would've rung as false to the woman as blame sense had.

"Don't use the word abduction." Bunyan chuckled. "You

may have come to America after Ernest's abduction—true use of the word—but Norwest Grind didn't grow from local franchise to global phenomenon until *after* you came."

"Oh. My. God." Evil slumped and facepalmed. "Clearly, Ernest's abductors timed pouring money into the Norwest Grind with my purchase because they knew your bias—the world's bias—against me would be strong enough to skip past the fact that some folks might just want a simple life. The real abductors could funnel money in, no matter where it tracked back to: drugs, terrorism, human trafficking, it would *make sense* since I was involved. Because my name is Evil and nothing is perceived as being below the Overlord family."

Evil felt himself falling into his emotions. His father would've slapped him by now, but—without that interruption —Evil finally nailed how he felt about his great-grandfather's legacy. Victimized.

He let those emotions show, too. "I'm the victim here twice over. First for trying to buy my way out of my old life. And, second, to your blind belief that everyone would choose to be super wealthy and rule over a country instead of a so-called nothing life of working at a coffee chain." Evil stood tall. "I wonder how many folks' choice would change after witnessing the deeds of a person who rules over a country he created with an iron fist and the other actions of someone capable of global mass genocide."

Evil tried to shrug off the his feeling, but couldn't. "If I go back, I become the monster that they want me to be. If I go into hiding somewhere else in the world, you and people like you hunt me like the monster that you all think I am." His arms flapped helplessly at his side. "No matter where I go or what I do, I won't be able to find peace."

That was exactly how he felt. Evil had told himself that, purely, he hadn't gone back because his mother's only lasting gift to him was his freedom. However, the compassion she had nurtured in him made him not want to be part of the family business.

Bunyan's high mental voice went through the link. *Jesus, I don't think I can take this. He's fourteen and only wants a life most teens despise.*

Both men grumbled.

Icee sent, *It's a load of crap. Man up.*

Mustard sent, *Orders are orders.*

Follow through, John. Psygun agreed. Then in a message outside the link, directed solely to Bunyan, she added, *One of us can report this later.*

Okay, Cathy. Bunyan's expression hardened. *But this just feels very wrong.*

Psygun replied, *It is wrong, but for now...*

Evil respected Psygun's commitment to orders and her plan to report this unusual situation. His father had him to assign nicknames to enemies because real names tended to create sympathy for them. Still, she had his respect and—in favor of Cathy—Evil discarded the Psygun nickname that he had made for her.

Bunyan agreed, *For now.* Speaking, Bunyan said, "We'll take all of what you said under consideration. But, for now, we need to finish your processing." Bunyan reached up. The hatch that the collar had come out of opened up again. This time wider as a folded, shrink-wrapped yellow jumpsuit fell into his hands. He tossed it to Evil.

Evil caught it and tucked it under his arm. "Uh." His gaze flitted to Cathy, then back to Bunyan. "Do I change here?"

Cathy turned her back. *Let me know when he's done.*

Bunyan nodded.

Evil thought Americans were more uptight about people undressing in front of them. Then again, this was a prison. He kicked off his shoes and turned around as he took off his pants.

His silhouette on the wall did the same.

Intrigued, he waved his hand.

Almost in real time, the silhouette did the same.

Evil turned his attention to the seamless shrink wrap around the jumpsuit. He ripped into it and pulled the jumpsuit out. Though it looked smooth, it felt like denim.

No one mentioned his socks or underwear so he kept them on as he thumbed the jumpsuit's placket. It didn't open. Evil had thought it would flip open to reveal a zipper or buttons, but the placket was Velcro.

He admired the simplicity of it.

Given the myriad powers that an ultrahuman inmate may have, not having anything on the jumpsuit that could be weaponized was smart. There would've been fewer injuries and deaths if his country had implemented Velcro closings in their jails instead of zippers and buttons.

He stepped in, pulled it up, and shrugged it over his shoulders. If he was at full power, the bright yellow would look sharp against his black skin. Like a deadly yellow jacket. But the jumpsuit against his alien gray skin made him look sickly. He still had his compact muscle, but his arms looked like they should be bigger.

Through their link, Bunyan asked, *Can you reach the boss? Obviously, Evil has more access to his powers now than when he had the vest on.*

Faint midnight blue energy radiated from her head in a half dome that expanded out toward the rest of the building. A split second later, a direct wispy line extended from her forehead going almost directly up.

She had contacted Pauly and he was in the room above them or a floor farther up.

Cathy nodded ever so slightly. *Relaying now.*

Bunyan added, *Oh, you should probably relay everything,*

especially about the kid nullifying himself to hide from Supreme and not wanting to go home.

Cathy replied, *Already on it.*

And she was. Evil noted that she relayed it exactly as Bunyan requested; no extras, no edits. She was the epitome of the mindset he tried to instill in his Peacekeepers.

She winced. As though being dressed down, her gaze dropped to her feet. The line that had rippled slightly as it went up had massive vibrations coming down. Whatever Pauly was sending back, he was yelling.

Wait. Evil seized on not being able to hear Pauly. He was able to hear Cathy and all of the traffic through her telepathy, but not Pauly's response. The only way that could be was if he were using a different telepath to reply back, which wouldn't make sense if already communicating with one. Unless—Evil turned the idea over in his head. Unless Pauly was a telepath. Then it'd only be natural to send instead reaching out for a mental link.

Evil focused to hear.

Most of what Pauly sent was well obscured. Usually that's done by sending in almost unnoticeable mental whispers, but that wasn't the case. Pauly had serious skill at keeping other telepaths from knowing that he was transmitting. And, in the case of a strong telepath, keeping them from knowing what was said.

Evil managed to latch his thoughts onto the line and slice through in time to hear Pauly yell, *I don't care how young he's pretending to be! When I say 'feed him to the wolves', you feed him to the damn wolves!*

Accusation in his voice, Bunyan asked, "What are you doing?"

"Huh?" Evil blinked away his attachment to Cathy's telepathic signal.

Her gaze shot to Evil.

Evil continued to blink. Any telepathic proof that he had done anything was gone, but something about digging through Pauly's telepathic shielding made his own thoughts lethargic.

"Just now." Bunyan closed the distance between them with two large strides. "What were you just doing? I saw you. You dropped into the zone. You used a power."

"What?" Evil's voice sounded sluggish to his own ears. "No." He picked the wrong word. No wasn't an answer to Bunyan's question. Still sluggish, Evil lied, "Nothing. I didn't do anything."

"He's lying." Cathy leveled her finger at him as she leveled her accusation.

Evil said, "Wait."

Bunyan didn't. His huge hand landed on Evil's back and balled his jumpsuit. Like picking up a bag of groceries, he hauled Evil from the ground as the exterior wall slid open. Growing in size up to his full fifty-foot height, Bunyan strode Evil over to the male inmate area. Through the size ratio change, the big man's fingers performed articulations that kept hold of Evil until Bunyan had gripped him like a kid held an action figure.

Bunyan's head was bigger than him.

Senses catching up, Evil's empathy flared. He noted that the goodwill and sympathy that he had managed to build up in Bunyan dissipated to almost nothing. Bunyan felt like a complete fool. Not for having gone easy on him, but for letting it build to the point that he questioned orders and talked back. Luckily the big man didn't have malice toward Evil, just a renewed resolution to the job.

Rearing back and aiming high, Bunyan called, "Pull!" He then uncorked and launch Evil high into the air over the invisible pen.

Chapter Twelve

AMONGST WOLVES

SOME HUNDRED FEET in the air, Evil arced high in the sky. Height wise, he was well above the black buildings and their antenna. Up here, the air was fresh in an outdoorsy way.

Still rising, it felt like someone had grabbed onto his sides just below his armpits. Mustard's yellow mental energy formed telekinetic hands to catch him at the free-floating peak where gravity, if it could speak, would've said *you've gone far enough*.

Evil made no attempt to shirk the hands.

From up here, the layout of the nearby buildings closely matched what he had imagined from seeing the antennas. There were many more buildings, and all of them the same uniform black. Like naval destroyers, each building had several arrays of guns. Many of the smaller ones were mounted on adjustable arms anchored to cantilevers—some of which tracked him through the air—while the really big suckers that Evil had only seen on battleships remained idle on their large turrets.

The entire complex was rimmed with gun-mounted watchtowers with thick black walls. Razor wire chain-link fence hemmed the one road that cut through the desert landscape leading from here to where the road touched a highway in the distance, tucked between hills that didn't look entirely like natural formations. Out there, probably parallel to the highway, the fence spanned across the fake hills and horizon.

Someone yelled from below, "Let him splat!"

Most of the inmates were looking up at Evil.

"Yeah!" One of the women who sat with two others agreed. "Let him splat!"

Both pens started a chant of, "Let him splat. Let him splat. Let him splat."

Evil could see a few just looking up, not chanting, but they were the clear minority.

The telekinetic hands had him, but opened to let him plummet.

His guts felt like they jammed up between his lungs, and his lungs wanted out though his throat. His throat constricted tight as though they might make it.

The inmates cheered.

Evil almost started flying, but the telekinetic hands came down with him. They were ready to catch him.

Besides entertaining the inmates, Evil recognized this for what it was.

He was used to being tested by his father and, occasionally, by his great-grandfather. The guards were checking to if he had the power of flight or some other way to keep from plummeting to the ground.

Falling into the musty gym-bag smell, a tiny worry about Mustard not catching him in time and possibly splatting worked Evil's nerves. He had some of his power back, which meant that his skin's density and physical resiliency would probably keep him from too much harm, and his regeneration should have him back on his feet in a few hours.

The worry shrank some, but grew back as the ground came closer.

What if he didn't survive the fall?

Before the worry could win out, the hands grabbed ahold of Evil at Bunyan's fifty-foot height and—to the prisoners' disappointed groans—lowered him to the ground a few feet from the big man.

Not concerned with looking stupid, Evil reached his hands out into the distance between him and Bunyan to feel what kept the prisoners in.

A ding came from his collar and so did Jimmy's toneless voice as it said, "Step back. First warning." Several of the pendulum-mounted guns swiveled from over the top of the building to point at Evil. Delayed ever so slightly, Jimmy's voice also came from the unseen speakers on the surrounding buildings.

He brought his arm back.

The guns stayed for a second and then retracted back over the top.

Evil's TA dimmed the world slightly. He turned as it lit the inmates from the dim in varying intensity to correspond with their threat level. His TA also pulsed light from where the threats would come from on their bodies. There were a few whose eyes shone like they could project beams, but most threats resolved around hands: claws, palms, radiating light indicating blast powers.

Knuckles aglow, a gang of five NFL linemen-sized bruisers closed in on Evil. He hadn't done anything to cross anyone yet. They must've been the welcoming committee.

Evil eyed them as his TA highlighted the usual weak points on a male body in red; the groin and the eyes always lit the brightest. The one in the lead had an unusually highlighted right knee as well as the left side of his chest.

A slim man with long black hair came flipping forward

over them. Evil's TA lit the guy's mouth and long, braided black hair as major threats. The guy's alabaster skin also had a slightly less dangerous highlight.

The man's voice held too much bass. "What'd you do to get kicked out?"

This guy didn't recognize him from before? Of course not. Evil's skin was now gray, he had been wearing a falseface, and he was in a prison jumpsuit.

He felt a strong compulsion to recount the end of the conversation that took place between him and the guards in the building, and to spill his guts about being caught using his telepathy to spy on a secret conversation between Cathy and Pauly.

The guy's eyebrows were also braided, with the ends dangling down to his jawline. The eyebrow braids straightened out to the sides of the guy's head and he gritted his pearly white teeth.

Breath hot and funky, the guy commanded, "Tell me."

The words almost came from Evil's lips.

Struggling to resist the intensified power, Evil wanted to release a psionic blast to teach the guy a lesson about using powers on strangers. However, that would tip his hand and let everyone—prisoners and guards alike—know some of what he could do. The less they knew, the better. Though it was a show of a different kind, he chose to resist the manipulation.

Lips threatening to betray him and do as the braided man ordered, Evil said, "If you ask normally, I might say."

The guy's eyebrow braids relaxed.

The compulsion to talk eased.

The overabundance of bass left Braids' deep voice as he asked, "Well?"

Not having to single-mindedly resist the guy's power allowed Evil to think.

Uncertain of what kind of infraction would get an indoor

prisoner booted to the outside, Evil played for time and looked up over his shoulder at Bunyan.

Bunyan had his stink-eye on at full tilt.

As Bunyan shrank to being twelve feet tall, Evil's empathic abilities sensed both hurt and disappointment from the big man. Both of Bunyan's feelings turned into a reluctant sadness, like having to relinquish a pet to the pound. After seeing Bunyan at full height, Evil wondered if that was the smallest Bunyan *could* go or just the smallest he *would* go.

Standing between Bunyan and the two guards in black, Cathy radiated a similar regretful feeling.

Bunyan turned and started back to the building.

Icy and Mustard hustled away to catch up with the others guards in black as they loaded into the line of Humvees.

Cathy stood there. The faint midnight blue of her telepathy beamed to Evil. *How much did you hear?*

Evil thought about reacting to hearing her mental voice like the folk who do that body-freezing, deer-in-the-headlights pose as they glanced around like a cat trying to find the source of the voice. But she knew who he was, and telepathy was one of the well-known powers that ran in his family.

If he replied mentally, his telepathic signal would alert her to how much of his power had returned, which probably would dwarf anyone else with a collar on.

He adopted the stern passive stare that his father had often used on him. It was more of a you-should-know-better-than-to-ask look than flat-out disdain, but there was clearly contempt for the question.

She thought, *You can tell me or Commander Gantt, but he won't be so nice.*

About to ask who Commander Gantt was, the rebellious part of him that rose up to goad Pauly awoke at the mention of the name Gantt.

Presuming that Gantt was Pauly's last name, Evil said, "Do you really think that threat holds any weight with me? You know who I am. You know I've suffered worse."

Acting every bit of his father, Evil popped a sneer. "Besides, between me and Gantt, whose presence do you think bothers the other the most?" Evil still thought of the commander as Pauly, but used Gantt to not possibly be recognized as the prisoner who just came through and called the boss-man Pauly.

Cathy projected, *I'm trying to help you.*

Though Evil could feel that she was sincere, he kept the same look.

She shook her head at him. *Well, if you heard it all, you know what's coming next.* Walking away, she sent, *Good luck, kid.*

Chapter Thirteen

INTO THE FIRE

LOADED UP, only the sound of the Humvees' tires on the asphalt signaled their driving away.

With Bunyan, Cathy, and their strong emotions gone, Evil felt the hostility-rich tension from Braids and his crew.

Evil turned.

Many of the other inmates had started to close in to form that I-want-to-see-the-action, but not-too-close human wall that hemmed schoolyard fights. As though there was a wall behind Evil, they formed a half dome. Their murmurs, body heat, and earnest want for bloodshed radiated warmth like a muggy Ultrava night adding a thick layer of their musk to the air.

Someone behind Braids cracked his knuckles.

Braids made a show of looking to where Bunyan had gone into the building and to the empty space where the Humvees and guards had been.

"Okay, Indoor. Now that they're gone—" Braids tilted his head slightly. His eyebrows stiffened away from his face as he bore down with his power "What. Did. You. Do?"

Braids stepped closer with each word.

Each word felt like a sledgehammer. Banging. On. The brick wall. Of. Evil's. Psychic shields. And they. Kept. Coming.

It felt like the moment he had lost the battle with his dad. The moment before his mental barriers gave out. The moment before the most severe beating of his life. The one after which his father had clamped nullifiers on Evil so his regeneration worked at a slug's pace.

Evil tried. To hold. Back. To. Resist.

Braids. Kept. On. Pounding. Pounding. Pounding.

Evil's knees started to give.

Braids went up on his toes to lean over him. Just. As. Evil's. Father. Had.

His father's words echoed back. *Now. You. Pay.*

Evil bellowed, "Nooo!" He sprang up, driving the top of his forehead into Braids' brow with every ounce of strength he had. He released a psionic blast on contact and shoved the man.

Limp in the air, Braids was flung over his gang and into the crowd behind them.

Evil's vision blurred with rage. Every one of Braids' five gang members sort of reminded him of his father.

Unlike his father, they ran. Weaving into the crowd of prisoners that also reminded him of his father.

Evil stepped forward.

They all stepped back.

One guy had his father's build. His father's look.

Evil pointed at him. "You!" He sprang and missed.

The crowd broke.

The guy ran.

Evil chased him for a few steps. He stopped and yelled, "Come back here—" He snipped his sentence off before saying *Father*. That one wasn't his father. His father wouldn't have run.

The prisoners' eyes flicked between Evil and something on the ground just behind him. Many of them looked defensively wary as they eased back to distances matching their varying level of concern.

Breathing hate, Evil raked his gaze across them. Looking for his father. Searching for the one person, the one ultrahuman, worthy of receiving every iota of his burning wrath.

He scanned the field of inmates again and again.

His father wasn't here.

Evil's senses started to come back to him. Of course his father wasn't here. His father was locked away in his great-grandfather's vault. But, for a moment, it sure felt like his father was beating on him. Well, not quite. His father would've been raining blows on him while pounding at his will.

Evil glanced at the other location that also had the prisoners' attention.

Hair strewn about, Braids was laid out on the asphalt. His forehead looked mushy and—though a thick bruise was growing—slightly caved in. Bright red ultrahuman blood trickled from his ears forming a small puddle.

A part of Evil felt bad. His mother had been instructing him to treat everyone as the unique person they were. Don't carry grudges and don't presume the thoughts of all by the actions of one. And he had unleashed years of pent up rage for his father on someone else.

Trying to make the feeling pass, Evil jaded his thoughts as the right red trickle continued. *Shouldn't have pushed me, Braids.*

It didn't work. Sorrow for hurting the guy kept slowly growing in Evil.

The crowd in yellow parted as Evil started to walk to the far side of the prison area to the mini-American football field.

Guilt building, Evil wished he had a soccer ball to dribble as he walked to get his mind off the mushiness of Braids' forehead. Off the damage, probably quite permanent, that he had caused.

His father had taught him that there were actions and reactions. Causes and effects. Right now, Braids was feeling the effect for choosing to act against Evil—if he felt anything. According to his father's teachings, that would've been it. Everything that happened would be hung upon Braids' and his actions.

However, Evil's mother had taken both the action-and-reaction and cause-and-effect training of his father one step further. After action and reaction, there was fallout. After cause and effect, there was understanding.

Braids' brain damage, if he was still alive—Evil hoped he was—was the fallout.

And Evil understood.

He understood why his father wanted to focus on the other person's actions and why his mother wanted him to look beyond that stark, simplistic view of the world.

Evil said, "Sympathy." And he said it just like his mother would've. He had learned the word in school, but his mother had taught him the true meaning. And two levels of regret stacked on him. First, for not just telling Braids what he wanted to know. Second, larger, but equally unchangeable, his running away with his mother.

If he would've stayed in his country, in his city, he wouldn't have his crushing guilt, as guilt—according to his father—was for the guilty. And, as rulers and ultrahumans, he, his father, and his great-grandfather were always in the right.

His mother had shown him that there was more to the world than that, and there was more to right and wrong.

Evil sighed.

A ding came from his collar; so did Jimmy's toneless voice. "Step back. Second warning in ten minutes."

Evil stepped back and looked up at the black buildings.

Guns had come over the edge and were pointed at him. Wondering what would happen on a third warning, and not wanting to find out from being pushed, Evil checked to make sure an inmate hadn't followed him to shove him out.

No one was there.

But, over in the women's section, the fifth woman who had been sitting crossed-legged was standing at the closest point.

Trying not to project ill will, Evil wondered what she wanted.

Her collar ding twice in rapid succession as she found the closest point in the women's area in which to sit cross-legged with her elbows tucked to her sides.

The start of Jimmy's toneless warning sounded like a DJ had scratched a record.

She looked at Evil with her passive expression.

Keeping the hundred feet between the two pens in mind, Evil walked toward her and asked, "What?"

She smiled an oddly familiar wide, bright smile. "Wasn't sure when I'd see you again, Ev."

Chapter Fourteen

WHAT'S IN A NAME

EVIL'S THOUGHTS went back to the last time someone had called him his old school nickname. It was the day before he and his mother left Ultrava and the Primazone.

Maria and Poobo, two of Evil's classmates that he'd chosen to bring in to the inner circle of his city's leadership, had just finished their final tests and each had earned the position of *Teniente de Bloque*. As Block Lieutenants, they were now in charge of everything that happened on a city block. A position that Evil's father had put him in three years prior, calling it leadership with training wheels.

During their training for an official position, they had to call him Evil Overlord just like his other officials. However, after Evil had issued them their symbolic TB shoulder patches and steel TB insignia for their dress uniforms, and the words of the national anthem had been sung, Maria had whispered over the closing music, "I won't fail you, Ev."

Poobo had whisper-corrected, "*We* won't fail you, Ev."

It had felt good to have both budding leaders his own age and to have friends who would call him—even only in hushed tones—what he preferred to be called.

Only his schoolmates had called him Ev, and hearing it brought a fond smile to his face. Even in the midst of this musty, wall-less pen hemmed by black buildings, the nickname sliced through his brooding.

Evil tromped the smile down to a suspicious glare. Hearing it from someone who was old enough to be one of his teachers was entirely at odds with the near instant classmate comradery it stoked in him.

He asked, "How do you know my name?"

An incredulous expression stole over her face. *"You're* questioning *me?"*

Her voice wasn't even familiar.

Evil said, "You bet." His own expression had gone skeptical as he searched her face and failed to find any similarity to anyone he knew.

He added. "One hundred percent."

Her eyelids fluttered as she rolled her eyes. "Am I that forgettable?"

"Lady." Evil crossed his arms and set his will against friendliness. "I don't know you."

Taken aback, she said, "Lady?" Then she rolled her eyes again and smacked her forehead. "That's right. Sorry. Forgot." She glanced around.

Reflexively, Evil did, too. No one was near them, but most of the inmates were watching.

"How about—" She touched her throat and her voice changed a bit to become more girly. "Now?"

There was a familiar sound, but Evil shrugged it off as he shook his head.

She looked around again before putting her hand up to shield the others' view of her face. Her forehead skin melded to two words that slowly formed in the bone beneath. They read, *It's me.* The *e* stayed while the others went flat and new letters came up. *Lupe.*

Evil's familiar smile sprang back as his mouth open a bit in true surprise.

"Lu—" Evil stopped himself from saying her real name. "Lucy." He corrected and sat on the warm asphalt to be on the same eye level with her. "How'd you end up here?"

The letters went flat as she motioned her head toward the others. "I won't go into all the details, but I was caught in a sweep by the authorities and was placed in jail until I told them my name." She didn't say *American* authorities, but that didn't need to be said.

Evil waited for her to answer the question that was on his mind. He didn't ask it because—as the daughter of two ultra-level precogs—Lupe tended to answer short questions before they were asked. But she didn't. Evil then remembered that she was adopted, was only a minor precog, and—more importantly—that both of them were wearing inhibitors. Since his minor powers were nerfed, he felt silly for expecting her minor power to work.

He asked, "Did you?"

"Tell them my name?" Her incredulous expression returned. "Of course not." She smiled. "They didn't know I had powers, but found out when they caught me during an escape attempt." She then motioned to her yellow jumpsuit. "The locals then sent me here." She bopped her head around on her shoulders. "It's been about two years."

"Two years?" Evil almost yelled. He thought about all the freedom he'd had for the last two years compared to this.

"Yup." Lupe bopped her head in that affirmative way she used when answering an unasked question. "There were some *big changes* a couple of years ago. *A lot* happened after..." She trailed off and blocked the side of her face again. *You left.*

Evil was going to ask *that bad*, but waited for her to answer. Then, again, remembered the inhibitors.

He asked, "Did it get that bad?"

Lupe's hand left her thigh to thumb a rock that stuck up from the asphalt more than the others. Her expressions faded as her gaze went there, too.

He waited, but she didn't answer.

Finally, not looking up, she said, "Well, I'm sure you know that caused the world to change."

Boy, did it. Evil knew what his father did to the world, but had no idea what was done in their country.

Not knowing what else to say, Evil said, "Sorry."

"S'okay." Lupe mustered a small smile. "Now that you're here, things are going to change for the better for both of us."

Evil couldn't imagine how. He asked, "Really?"

"Yes." She gave a quick, sure nod. "I've seen it."

Chapter Fifteen

THAT FAMILIAR FEELING

THERE HAD BEEN many times in Evil's life when he wanted to have the power of precognition. While his father pined for it to be able to outmaneuver his enemies, Evil would've been happy with just the tiniest level.

A few seconds of future insight could change the course of conversations and give him the precious ability to change his mind or to say something else or just remain silent. The part of him who coveted the ability wondered how this entire prison thing would've gone differently if he hadn't mouthed off to Pauly.

Lupe looked toward the others.

"Clear the area." Guards dressed in black at the heavily populated part of the men's section gave the order to inmates over there. Bunyan towered over them. "Clear the area."

The inmates did.

Mustard-yellow telekinetic hands lifted the still unconscious Braids above the crowd and pulled him straight out of the pen.

Guns swiveled over the sides of the buildings, pointed at Braids as Jimmy's toneless voice issued a warning. A moment later, the guns flipped back over the tops of the buildings and out of sight again.

The telekinetic hands carried Braids to the black building Evil had been in.

Pauly, Bunyan, and six guards in black came walking down the wide distance between the two pens.

Lupe whispered, "Control yourself."

Though Evil felt a little down about what he had done to Braids, he didn't feel any remnants of the emotional state that made him lash out. Wondering why she would say that, he glanced at her.

Even quieter, she whispered, "Don't talk back."

Remembering the sudden outburst from deep within himself, Evil's eyes widened in realization of what Lupe was warning him about. He gave a small appreciative nod.

Getting closer, Pauly pointed over his shoulders to Braids and said, "Surveillance tells me that you did that."

The rebellious feeling woke up.

Evil pressed his lips tightly together to keep control of his mouth. He nodded.

Bunyan spoke to Lupe. "Back up."

Lupe got up and took exactly two steps back.

Pauly came to a stop right in front of Evil. Bunyan stood behind him while three guards lined Pauly's left and right.

A soft murmur from Evil's left caught his attention.

The other inmates had ease over halfway down the pen to eavesdrop on the conversation.

Pauly put his hands behind his back and rocked in place. "Care to share why you did that?" His breath smelled of pastrami.

The rebellious feeling in him was anxious—frothing—waiting for Evil to open his mouth so that it could goad Pauly.

Evil kept his lips tight and shook his head.

Looking down at him, Pauly chided, "What, you don't want to say anything?"

Evil tamped the rebellious feeling and shook his head.

"Well." Pauly picked imaginary lint from a shoulder. "Doesn't really matter. Surveillance says Robins and his boys looked like they were going to give you *the rules*—" Pauly used air quotes. "When you rocket head-butted him." Pauly shrugged in that careless fashion that Evil didn't know at all, but it infuriated the rebellious part of him. Pauly smacked his lips like he was tasting the delicious smelling pastrami that was on his breath.

Another annoying mannerism that infuriated the rebellious streak.

Pauly continued, "So, instead of being the one broken and bleeding, it looks like you've taken one of these assholes off of my hands. And for that, I thank you." Pauly gave him a slight bow. "However, you made no friends in doing that and you're going to have to sleep sometime."

Evil glanced at the inmates looming a ways off. Though he wondered if they all slept on the ground, he didn't risk opening his mouth to ask.

Pauly got one more piece of lint from his other shoulder before putting his hands behind his back. "However, I'll make you a deal. Tell me where you got that vest from and I'll section you off a safety zone. It won't be as good as having your own cell inside, but you could rest better knowing the guns will cut down anyone who tries to get you while you're sleeping."

Evil wasn't going to give up Jimmy, but he could use the name of one of the tech conglomerates that had set up in the Primazone and only sold to the government. However, Lupe had warned him to keep quiet and there was no telling what the rebellious part of him would say.

Tired of it pinging around in him, threatening to hijack

anything he said, Evil focused on the feeling to try and understand what caused—

Still sitting, Evil's eyes rolled back in his head.

It was New Year's 2000. Everyone was worried about Y2K —whatever that was—*and Pauly had her*—her?—*head out to their self-sufficient cabin up in Lake Tahoe to be out of any major cities in case the turn of the millennia caused havoc. He was going to meet her there.*

To bring in the New Year in their usual way. She had followed her mother-in-law's recipe to make authentic lasagna with the chunks of Italian sausage that Pauly liked in the layers. She had made sure some would be visible through the glass dish as it sat on an oven mitt in the center of the table. Unable to find the celebratory candles, she had used a couple of packs from the cupboard and set them around the room to really set the mood.

Pauly had come in. He'd looked haggard from the road. Before she could ask about his day, his eyes had bulged at the numerous lit candles. His belt cleared his loops with dreadful snaps. He railed about wasting the survival candles while taking the belt to her.

It was the time she had discovered her power. Somehow, she was able to press air against the belt to slow it just before it landed on her skin, again and again.

He was out of control. If she hadn't had the ability, she would've needed to go to the hospital.

Instead, after Y2K turned out to not be a big thing, he'd had her stay in Tahoe until her welts healed.

She used that time to nudge dust. Over the years, she had used the ability to lessen beatings until one night, when she had had enough of his abuse, she discovered that she could lift herself and stay up in the air. She could fly and she was leaving.

But he was there. In her head. He was a telepath!

Pauly tried to soothe her. Asked her, begged her, not to leave. He'd do better. He'd change.

She had heard the words before and when she refused to stay until he got home so they could talk it out, he'd commanded her, stepped on her will, and made her.

EVIL BLINKED BACK to reality and shook the weight of her hate in his head. He knew. He understood. The reason the rebellion was so strong was that it was in defense of herself from Pauly that Deborah—the woman he had absorbed what he thought was flight from—had developed and honed her power of air control.

Pauly said, "Come on." Pauly pantomimed holding a putter and knocking a ball. His blue eyes followed an imaginary ball rolling away. "Just give in and give me this piece of intel and your life gets easier."

Under his own compunction, Evil said, "Or what? You're going to beat me like you did your wife?"

Lupe groaned. *"Santa Maria."*

Chapter Sixteen

STOKING FLAMES

THE REBELLIOUS FEELING deep in Evil thrilled with pleasure and then, as Pauly's face reddened to a pomegranate, it shrank slightly at the thought of facing Pauly's inner demon, but only for a moment. It rebounded back to being full-on defiant.

The smell of pastrami reminded Evil that he hadn't eaten for a bit. With his resiliency back, Evil wouldn't have to eat for a long while, but he still had the want.

Evil stood and pointed off in the direction Pauly had faked a putt. He said, "I think you missed."

Pauly straightened up and stared at Evil. The red of his skin had been the typical Caucasian-getting-angry body flush, but the pupils of his eyes flicked red. A battalion of hate marched in his eyes. Pauly's jaw tightened, veins bulged in his neck as two thick ones spidered up his forehead.

Grinning at Pauly barely keeping it together, Evil goaded, "Can your inner demon come out to play?"

Evil took a lazy step back and motioned a challenge for Pauly to step into the pen and close the distance to fight.

Spittle seeped from Pauly's tight lips. The landscape of his teeth behind them shifted as though they had grown in length and doubled in number.

Evil gave one last poke. "Why don't you go get your belt first?"

Pauly's blue eyeballs burst into flame. The white of his eyes turned to rolling yellow. The blue irises turned white-hot with a licking red pupil.

Bunyan grabbed Pauly and grew to his full height in an instant. Using the momentum of the sudden growth along with his increased strength, Bunyan chucked Pauly over the roof of one of the black southern buildings with enough force that Pauly would probably clear a couple of rows.

"Soldiers. North." Bunyan pointed north and urged. "Go! Go! Go!"

Bunyan went directly south. Thoughts rippled faint midnight blue from the big man's head and spread out eight directions down a mental link as the giant ran to the black building, leapt up to grab the ledge, and like a kid climbing a wall, hoisted himself up and over.

Bunyan sent, *Unions, we have a code fireball in south two or south three.*

Answers came back.

On it. That was Icee's mental voice.

On it.

Coming.

On it. Cathy's mental voice.

FB confirmed in south three. Mustard's mental voice.

En route.

Bunyan's mental voice ordered over two others checking in. *Someone shutdown surveillance and sound cover.*

Mustard replied, *Done, and...*

At double speed, Jimmy's toneless voice rattled orders from the speakers. "BT one through eight, n-e-fifteen-eight. CT one through four, o-n-u-three. CT five through nine, o-s-d-seven—" Jimmy continued as guards in black and camo uniforms poured from the buildings.

The black guards tore off on foot running north.

The camo guards hopped into the camo Humvees that sped in. As soon as four got in, the vehicle sped northward.

Still at double speed, Jimmy began to repeat the orders. "BT one through..."

Evil focused his telepathy on the guards still scrambling from the building and hustling away on foot or in Humvee.

Most were, in one form or another, annoyed at their day being interrupted by scenario drills. Some were steeling themselves in case this wasn't just a drill. Some were excited for something finally happening to break up the monotony, and a few were looking forward to using their weapons.

If any of the guards paid any attention to the pens, it was nothing more than a cursory glance to make sure there wasn't a prison break before heading north.

Evil thought about Bunyan calling orders to turn off surveillance and sound cover, and Mustard replying that it was done.

Alert for movement—for guns—on the rooftop, Evil prepared to hop back as he eased over to where Pauly had fake putted.

No movement.

No guns.

Evil rushed the hundred feet over to Lupe. "Grab on. I'll fly us out of here." She used to always have the faint smell of light myrrh. Now she smelled funky, like any other prisoner.

"No." She shook her head. "This isn't how we escape."

Evil asked, "What?"

Lupe glanced around.

Other prisoners started to cross the unseen parameters. They inched farther and farther, all the while watching the roofs.

One guy jogged east.

Then another.

And a few more.

Evil urged, "Come on. We can escape in the chaos."

Lupe rattled an explanation. "If we go now, you'll never get the freedom you want. Not only that, but the freedom we do gain will only be temporary."

Evil asked, "Temp—"

"Yes," she cut in, answering before he got the question out. "Temporary, as in we'll both be abducted back to the Primazone in a few months and I'll never get home."

Whoa. Evil asked, "As in, you'll be killed on the way and never make it to your parents?"

Lupe shook her head, "No. Like, I'll never get home to my dimension."

"What?" Evil struggled with her regressing to that sort of crazy talk she used to say in the first and second grades.

Four-Arms rushed to them. She yelled, "Now we'll see if I have to kill you." She was focused on Lupe.

Evil stepped in front of Lupe and readied to fight Four-Arms.

The woman pivoted to run to the southeast. Her breakneck sprinting around the corner triggered many more prisoners to run. They ran wildly around the buildings to the east and west.

Lupe pushed on Evil's back to get him to walk toward the men's pen. "Just go back and wait."

Evil turned around.

Her hands landed on his chest and a thrill went through him as he walked backward. He resisted her direction just enough so she would continue pushing on him.

Lupe pushed him to the edge of the women's pen.

Evil set himself.

Her hands went flat against his chest. Feeling.

He flexed.

She recoiled and blushed. “If you want to be free, really free, you’ll go back and wait.”

Smiling—was he flirting with her? felt like it—Evil asked, “You’ve foreseen this?”

She was still blushing. “No. Jorge and Yazmine prepared me for this moment, insisting that if you leave now, I don’t leave with you.”

Lupe dropping the names of two ultra-level precogs—her adoptive parents—bolstered Evil’s faith that this would be the right move. Their predictions were the only things that swayed his great-grandfather’s actions.

Evil wanted his freedom, but he stopped and walked back to Lupe. He asked, “If I were to leave, would you come with me?”

Lupe’s blushing intensified. She didn’t back up as he stepped into her personal space. She looked into his eyes and breathed, “Yes.”

He touched under her chin to urge her forward and he leaned in.

She came forward.

They kissed.

Something flicked on in Evil. He’d been aroused before, but this was something different. Something with substance. Something...real.

She pulled back slightly and asked, “Will you wait?”

Evil snuck a peck. “Ten seconds ago, I would’ve said no.” He nodded to her as he started to walk backward out of the women’s pen. “But that was then.”

Lupe smiled her lovely smile.

Now, Evil could see the girl he knew in the woman’s face. A possibility that woman might be her true form and she was just pretending to be a kid in the Primazone struck him.

While kind of creepy, the possibility of getting with a grown woman was kind of hot.

He stopped. "Wait. Are you really fourteen?"

"Yazmine told me you would ask, horn dog." She covered her reddening face and laughed at him through her hands. "Yes, I'm fourteen."

Evil grinned. He continued back until he was in the men's section.

He asked, "How much did she tell you about this moment?"

Lupe gushed and grinned. "Enough."

"Okay." In case his estimation was off, Evil adjusted where he stood to be just a little farther in the men's area. "I'll wait to see what happens next." He grinned and it felt stupid and awkward. He slipped a double entendre. "It better be good."

Lupe said, "It'll be worth it."

Her word play sent another thrill through him. Under his breath, Evil whispered, *"Santa Maria."*

Chapter Seventeen

PRISON BREAK

Of the two hundred plus male prisoners, less than twenty remained and Lupe was the only woman in the female pen. With most prisoners gone, the smell on the air went from neglected gym bag down to a lone pair of dirty sox.

A few scattered gunshots lit from the north. Then the staccato of controlled full-auto bursts, and then—like a fuse had burned down to an endless string of firecrackers and M-os—shit really popped off.

As though searching, Lupe looked around her feet and laid facedown on the asphalt, looking Evil's way. She closed her eyes and, despite the growing mayhem around them, looked peaceful.

Lupe said, "Get down. Bullets are going to start strafing this area."

About to get down, Evil noticed that many of the remaining prisoners had dropped flat on the ground. She hadn't yelled it, but they had reacted. One of them, a guy with wild, shoulder-length, bright green hair, was whispering directions to the rest.

Unable to hear exactly what was said, Evil hooked into Green Hair's thoughts.

The guy had enhanced hearing, had full faith in whatever Lupe said, and was focused on listening to her for further advice to survive the day. More than that, Green Hair hoped to be able to piggyback on their plan to attain some of that true freedom that she had mentioned.

Evil's TA advised him to twist and bend. He did and a group of bullets whizzed by.

Offended that Green Hair had spied on Lupe's warning, Evil sent her a mental whisper. *There's a guy here with heightened hearing. He knows that we're waiting for something.*

Lupe whispered, "I know." Her voice lowered and was barely audible between the gunshots. "Listen very closely." She covered her ears and winked.

Evil's TA warned him to do likewise. He did.

Two riotous booms came from a building behind him. The sound reverberated on his skin and had to be murder to anyone with heightened hearing.

Evil to see what the guns had fired at.

Two faint trails went from one of the barely visible barrels of the building's battleship guns. Evil's gaze raced along the thickening trails where the round hit something in the air and shattered into light like a roman candled.

From the explosion point in the sky, a person fell.

Evil shook his head. "Poor decision." Admonishing the flyer for venturing above the buildings, Evil could only watch him—or her—plummet.

Limp, the body came straight down in the distance.

Buildings blocked the view of the impact with the earth.

High-pitched alarms sounded. Jimmy's voice, not toneless but still obviously recorded, alerted. "Code yellow. Code yellow. We have a code yellow." And went on repeat.

Green Hair writhed and flopped on the ground, clutching

his ears. Blood seeped from between his fingers.

Evil occasionally twisted to dodge bullets as his TA advised.

Many of the arm-mounted swivel guns on roofs popped up.

He twitched. Keen on his TA.

The guns didn't hook over the side to point at him. They pointed at various distant targets to the east and west, and started cracking off shots in perfect three-round bursts.

Lupe said, "I know. That's why I didn't say your name." She added, "And I'm grateful that you didn't use mine." Her eyes widened. "Get down. For real!" She slapped the asphalt. "Get down!"

Evil took a knee and was about to lie down slowly when his TA alerted him that he wasn't moving fast enough.

He flopped on his face.

A deep gong sound filled the area as bright white light cast strong shadows beneath him.

Evil consulted his TA to know if it was safe to roll over. It was. He did.

Like looking up into a solid sheet of florescent lighting, a blanket of light was projected from all surrounding buildings. The plane of light was two feet from the ground and covered everything from one building to the others.

If anyone had been standing, this unknown energy would've struck them about mid-thigh.

Evil wanted to know what the energy was and what it did, but he wasn't curious enough to reach out and touch it. Well, he was that curious, but his TA warned him against it, so he kept his hand against his body. Waiting for the lights to dim, he closed his eyes and rolled back over. But it didn't.

Neither did the gunfire.

Another battleship gun didn't sound again, but the occasional *shunk* and *thoom* from mortars sounded above the firefight happening throughout the complex, as did the *whoosh* and explosion of a rocket launcher.

On top of the sounds of conventional war were the sounds powers of escaping ultrahumans. Someone out there had an impressive level of sound manipulation magnifying their claps into battering cones of sound. Well, Evil presumed they were battering as the sound of crumpling, twisted metal usually came right on the heels of the ultra-claps.

Evil asked, "Lu—" He almost said her name again. "Lucy, how much longer?"

She answered, "The light, a few more minutes. The fight, a little more after that."

Evil appreciated the information, but it wasn't what he was asking. He projected his thoughts to her. *I mean, how much longer until we're free?*

She replied, "A couple of hours, but I have to confess something to you, Ev."

Evil projected, *Yeah?* He could feel building sorrow radiating from her. Why? Sheltering his lower eye with a hand, Evil opened it to look at her. Her eyes were clamped tight and turmoil twisted her facial expression.

"While there is a chance for true freedom, it's just a chance." She paused and swallowed. "And it's a pretty small one."

A small chance? The thought struck him. He had held off on escaping because she dropped the names of two highly esteemed precogs. Precogs who, despite other precogs modifying outcomes, each had well over a ninety-five percent accuracy rating. Lupe hadn't given him a proper promise, but using their names virtually guaranteed whatever predictions they made...

The feeling of betrayal started to re-frame her story in his mind. Evil couldn't take it. Mentally, and physically, he yelled, "What?"

Chapter Eighteen

FALLOUT

EVIL PROJECTED, *Tell me you're only saying that for anyone who may be listening.*

Lupe's face tightened. Sorrow laced her guilt.

Evil's vigor left him. His body felt numb. They had had a moment. A connection, and she had used that. Used that to get him to stay so that she could get to her supposed home dimension.

His father and great-grandfather often had Evil execute plans without telling him the real reason or sharing the big picture. All of his life, up to his running away to America with his mom, Evil had been used. Heck, after this twist, Evil wasn't even sure if his mother's intentions were as pure as getting him away from his father. Evil often felt her resentment for his father. She could've talked him into running away as a way of striking back at his father—an ultrahuman who way out-classed her.

Evil's TA advised him to move. Numb, he didn't want to, but did. Just enough.

A giant boot—Bunyan's boot—came stepping through the light.

Bunyan bellowed and mentally screamed.

The bright plane of light flicked out.

Bunyan swooned as his body smoked. His eyes rolled in his head.

Evil TA's went off again. He popped up to his feet and leapt clear of the big man as he came smacking down on the asphalt like a face-planted skater.

Normal size skulls whacking against the ground made most feel uneasy. Evil had been deadened to it for years. However, the sound of Bunyan's massive noggin made Evil cringe. He didn't care for the big man in particular, but that sound along with Bunyan reeking of burnt hair and flesh had Evil wondering if the big guy would survive.

Bunyan's body blocked his view of Lupe.

And Evil was glad. He didn't want to see her right now.

Then he noticed how Bunyan was lying and, accounting for the ratios, the big man had fallen where she had laid down.

Against his conscious anger at her, Evil wonder if Lupe was okay. He was furious with her and was surprised to find that he still cared about her well-being. He used his telepathy as a close-range radar and picked up her and Bunyan's mental signatures. She was alive and the type of pain she felt was either mental or emotional. Bunyan was alive, but unconscious.

A warbling screech came from the corner of the building Four-Arms had run around. Pauly stood there. He had transformed. Muscle-bound, his skin was the color of an eggplant, and dark amethyst light pulsed from him. His ears rose into points above his head, bony knobs lined the top of his forehead, and his cheeks jutted out slightly above a second set of fiery eyes. All of his eyes were fixed on Evil.

Demon-Pauly screeched, "You wanted my inner demon, Evil Overlord?" Mocking what Evil had done a bit ago,

Demon-Pauly took a lazy step back and motioned a challenge for Evil to close the distance to fight. "Come. Face me."

Murmurs came from the remaining prisoners, but Evil kept his focus on Demon-Pauly. His TA lit the purple skin as dangerous, the black-clawed hands as perilous. Heck, even Demon-Pauly's eyes and mouth were marked as hazardous. Though Evil waited, his TA didn't light any weaknesses. As when facing down his father—who was more powerful—Evil's TA told him to back away. To run.

His TA then warned about a much lesser danger, not a threat, coming up from behind him.

Evil spun.

A prisoner who looked sort of familiar—not famous like Bunyan, but like someone Evil had known—rushed him. Flesh was layered over where his eyes should've been, but still he knew the man.

Evil guessed, "Pilgrim?"

Pilgrim's forever humbled voice came out as rich as Evil remembered. "I mean you no harm, sire." Hope radiated from him.

"What happened to your eyes?" Confident that his TA would trigger if Pilgrim attacked, Evil turned back to Demon-Pauly. Besides, seeing one of his old bodyguards like that was unnerving.

"What?" Pauly continued to wave him over. "Scared?"

A little. When Evil had felt this out-classed against his father, his pent-up anger at always being told what to do had made him attack. Back then, deep down, Evil hadn't thought his father would kill him if he lost. Not so with Demon-Pauly.

"Supreme." Pilgrim explained, "Since I had failed in my one purpose, he took my eyes and my name."

Evil nodded. He never understood his great-grandfather's punishments. They were always odd and never in line with what was done. Worse, the penalty always out-weighed the infraction.

In fact, given how his great-grandfather was, it was miraculous that Pilgrim was still alive and had enough power in him to warrant being in a prison like this. That was something Evil had been taught never to do. If an ultrahuman failed badly enough, they were to be stripped of their powers and killed.

Evil said, "Sorry to hear that." Knowing that it was going to suck and probably wouldn't go well, Evil summoned the courage to go face Demon-Pauly. While he didn't like the man, the only way to quiet the part of him that had a personal history with Pauly was to beat his demon form down. That should satisfy the rebellious streak and put Evil fully back in control of his body and powers.

"But I'm still alive," Pilgrim said. "He named me Heretic."

Though Evil had asked Pilgrim a question, the man tended to talk and talk. Evil didn't want to ignore him, but he had to focus on his TA to find the best way to approach and fight the demon.

Pilgrim's hope turned reverent. "And I still serve."

From behind, there was pressure against Evil's collar and then a sharp sound like metal being snipped.

Pilgrim's hope rapidly blossomed to joy. "And I'm going to have my vision back. And my name."

Evil's collar fell from his neck. Surprised, he caught what remained of it as it turned to ash in his hands. Like a heat sensitive mug reacting to being filled with coffee, the alien gray color of his skin started to darken as Evil felt his powers —all of his powers—begin to ramp up.

Pilgrim raised his voice in praise. "I will see again, I will see again. Lord above, I will see again."

Evil turned his focus back to the demon.

The weight of his great-grandfather's suffocating mental voice filled his head. *Found you.*

Dread crashed down upon Evil. Though he could move, he felt rooted to the ground. No matter where he went, without nullification, his great-grandfather would be able to lock onto his mental signature. Evil despaired. How could he get away?

Chapter Nineteen

POWER UP!

GUNSHOTS STILL REPORTED in the distance. Bunyan uttered a small groan, twitched, and went still again. The smell of his burnt hair started to get into Evil's nose and weigh on his tongue like he had licked charcoal.

"You're finally conscious." His great-grandfather sounded relieved, verging on joy. "And you're stronger." He commanded, "Get safe and wait for me, Evil. I'll be there in a jiffy to bring you back home."

With his great-grandfather pinpointing where he was, Evil knew it was only a matter of a few minutes—or however long it took the royal teleporter to lock in on the location—before his great-grandfather mounted what he probably thought was a rescue.

Evil had to get his vest. Yes. He had to get his vest, steal a vehicle, and put his vest back on so he couldn't be tracked by his great-grandfather. That, or at least get a collar. A collar. Yes. Then zoom away and set up a rendezvous with Jimmy to get another vest.

"I will see again." A thread of concern laced into Pilgrim's joyous song. "But I have to see to my seeing again."

Since Bunyan was out, Evil thought about sending a telepathic request to Cathy for a collar, but his great-grandfather would surely hear it.

Evil looked at Demon and hoped to appeal to what remained of Pauly. "My great-grandfather is coming, Pauly."

"Pauly's asleep." The demon started to walk forward. "And I don't care."

Evil said, "I need a collar or he's going to destroy this place and everyone in it."

"Don't." Demon extended his arms and curled his fingers. "Care." Flaming, black-fire claws—not claws, psionic energy looking like fire—the length of his fingers projected from Demon's claws. "Really don't."

Evil's TA warned against the demon's actual claws and hands. Though the flame-claws looked wicked, Evil's mental defenses would probably render them less effective than Pauly was used to.

Also, with Evil's powers coming back, his TA no longer told him to run away; it still suggested it, but the threat from Demon was no longer totally overwhelming.

The best way to fight fire-based ultrahumans was with cold. Powering up a blast, Evil focused his cryokinesis on his hands and fused it with some of his telepathic might. Frost billowed from his palms and the slight moisture around him turned into snowy crystals.

Evil's TA warned him about Pilgrim. He spun. "What the hell, man?"

"I'm loyal." Pilgrim was jogging backward, twisting his arms and waggling his fingers making Evil's power weaken. He sang, "You need to be here when Supreme comes."

"Pilgrim!" The cryoblast in Evil's hands remained as his absorbed powers went dormant. His TA winked out and his other naturalized powers began to soften. He let a cryoblast go at his former bodyguard.

The jet of ice flashed to Pilgrim, hit him, knocked him back, and froze him in a ten-foot ice sphere.

Evil spun back to face Demon. Without even a whiff of his TA, the world looked very different. Felt different. He no longer had the solid advantage that got him through most of his challenges. He no longer knew how he stacked up against Demon and lost all insight as to what would be the best move.

He thought about releasing his last cryoblast, but what if Demon dodged?

Demon rolled his shoulders and started to jog toward Evil.

Instinctively going for higher ground, Evil ran up on Bunyan's hand and then along his arm to get to the big man's chest.

Dark amethyst flashed at Bunyan's shoulder. Demon appeared at the center of the flash. Swinging.

Evil stumbled back out of the way.

Demon pressed the attack.

Evil dodged by leaping back to the asphalt.

Claws leading, Demon jumped at him.

Evil sprang farther away and turned to blast.

Demon was there. Swinging. Striking.

The claws slashed down Evil's chest. The flame-claws turned to smoke as the real claws bopped down his ribs, tearing away skin and muscle.

Bellowing in pain, Evil punched Demon in the gut. He released his cryoblast.

Demon was encased in an ice sphere.

Looking at the gashes down his chest, Evil backed away. Blood welled from the wound and down his jumpsuit. He could feel his weakened regeneration work at healing the wound.

The pain made him want to close his eyes and lie down

until he was better. He struggled against that feeling and checked on Demon.

A crack formed in the ice sphere from Demon's forehead to the edge where a small steam geyser spouted.

Glancing around, Evil noticed that the remaining prisoners had bolted. The few guns that were visible were leading far off targets before occasionally releasing a shot. Besides the unconscious Bunyan, there were no guards in sight. All of the unions the big man had called must've all be out of commission.

Cracking ice returned Evil's attention to Demon.

Two more fractures appeared in the sphere from Demon's hands to the surface. More steam spewed. Soon the whole thing would shatter.

Evil lashed out with a bolt of mental power.

Demon's eyes twitched in pain. The steam slowed.

That attack normally knocked anyone but his father out. It hurt Demon, but he was still very much awake and pissed.

Evil sent another and another.

Demon winced with each. His eyes widened in rage. The sphere cracked in six more directions. Steam billowed as the sphere shrank slightly.

Evil summoned all of his telepathic might and drilled into Demon's psyche to find Pauly. The man could be reasoned with, but not the demon. He had to bring Pauly back to the surface, back into control.

Chapter Twenty

THROUGH FIRE

THE MENTAL LANDSCAPE of most minds was usually a mishmash of where the person grew up, where the person worked, where the person lived, and, sometimes, the way the person viewed the world with a dash of how they wished it would be.

Demon's and Pauly's minds were one and the same. Though the landscape was Pauly's skyrise version of some downtown city, the buildings, streets, and cars were wreathed in flame and an eye-stinging phosphorous reek hung in the sweltering air. Though the flaming city had unbelievable high-rises, Evil recognized the Bradbury Building that his mother had wanted to tour. Pauly's vision of L.A. was vastly different from reality.

Traveling into Demon's mind made Evil's physical pain vanish, but his mental self felt like it had been put in a pot of boiling water.

Evil raised his psychic shields and the heat lessened. The ground five feet around him extinguished to be regular city street. The air still stunk, but the constant cooking sensation ceased.

Encased in mental ice a hundred feet away, Demon glared at him. A muffled rumbling growl rolled down the street.

Evil made eye contact for a brief instant and then turned his attention to finding Pauly. Even if he were familiar with the landscape, he had no idea of where to look for Pauly. And if he did know, the flaming buildings made distinguishing one from another a dicey endeavor.

Faint diamond dust made the outline of a face with brilliant sapphires for eyes and butterfly wings for lips. The winged lips didn't move as a mental voice, not from Demon's mind but from Evil's, said, "Hello."

Evil said, "Hi." The last time he had heard that voice—Deborah's voice—she was begging for his father's mercy.

Deborah's outlined face turned upward as her eyes focused on a spot in a building. "That was our apartment. That's where he'll be."

Evil nodded and asked, "Can you still envision it?"

Her face gave an uncertain nod. "Parts."

Evil said, "Focus on the strongest image."

Her sapphire eyes closed. She gave a nod.

Evil touched her face.

A stove she had cooked at—and burned upon—many times appeared in front of them. Then a frig to their right and the open living room, which spilled into the den, which had a commanding view of the burning city. Nothing in the apartment was on fire.

The sounds of an American football game came from the den.

Pauly said, "Babe, while you're in there, bring me a beer."

"Yes, dear." The diamond dust that outlined her face thinned to spread out to form her body. She opened the refrigerator, whose interior spanned fifty feet in the distance. The shelves were stocked with prime cuts of steaks of all sorts. The door shelves were crammed full of twelve-ounce

Miller High Life bottles, and two things happened when she pulled one: another bottled instantly filled the spot and the bottle she pulled morphed into a forty-ounce bottle.

Evil extended his hand for it.

Fear filled her sapphire eyes; she shook her head and walked it into the dining room.

Evil followed.

Coliseum stairs led up to a super-sized La-Z-Boy where a Bunyan-sized Pauly sat in front of a Jumbotron-sized TV, rooting for the Rams as they walked all over a team in black and gold with a white dot on their black helmets. The score was 124 to 3.

Deborah and the bottle shrank in size as she made her way up the stairs. She had to climb the last one like it was a six-foot wall. When Pauly took the bottle, it grew into a Bunyan-sized forty ounces again.

Pauly said, "A steak would be nice."

Deborah said, "Yes, dear," and started to come back down the stairs.

Hoping to broker goodwill, Evil addressed Pauly with his title. "Commander Gantt."

Pauly's neck popped when he whipped his head to glare at Evil. "You!"

"Me." Evil nodded. "You need to take control. The Demon-You is going to get your compound destroyed."

Pauly stood and grew taller. "What are you doing in my house?" He stared at Deborah as she rushed to get down the last few steps. "Are you having an affair, woman?" His huge hand reached out for her.

Deborah cried as she sprinted.

Evil raised his hands and projected a protective dome around Deborah. As much as Evil tried to change it, his energy on the mental plane always looked like bubbles, a childhood joy of his.

Pauly yelled, "My house! My wife! My rules!"

Evil focused on Pauly to sap some of his might. The man instantly shrank to normal size. Given how much mental power Evil thought the man had, that should've been a massive mental struggle, but it was cake.

Pauly looked to Deborah and tried to soothe her. "You know I would never hurt you, baby. Never."

It sounded and resonated like a lie.

Deborah was full of mistrust.

Pauly faced Evil and yelled, "Get out of my house! Get out of my head!"

Those two commands should've been enough to make Evil fight to stay present and active, but it was like Pauly didn't have any mental powers at all.

Pauly doesn't have mental powers. The realization made Evil grab his forehead. There were two personalities in here and the other one—Demon—had wrestled all power from Pauly. Clearly, Pauly wasn't the dominant personality keeping the wild one in check. Demon used Pauly as a mask.

Evil projected his mental self back to the flaming street where Demon should've been. Only large chunks of melting ice remained.

A powerful scaled hand appeared out of the air before Evil and grabbed him hard by the neck. Demon's white-fire eyes appeared as strong as the sun.

Demon's sneering grin was equally blinding. "Since you took a trip in my mind, I'm going into yours."

The intensity of his eyes became eclipsed by inky blackness. Tar's mental trap set deep in Evil's psyche was triggered. The darkness rained in icy cold splotches on the flaming city, snuffing it out. The black began to fill the streets like a flash flood of arctic water.

Inside of the offender's mind, the fluid black turned to thick morass covering Evil, gluing him ankle deep to the spot.

His feet went numb.

He tried to yank against it to pull free, to get back to his own head, but the ink had become tar and now was up to his mid-calves.

To his knees.

Mid-thighs.

Evil made a mental bar anchored in the air above him.

The black coated it.

Waist deep.

Evil grabbed on.

Chest deep.

He pulled. No results.

A set of phantom hands grabbed onto each of Evil's wrists.

Armpit deep.

He felt amped up.

Neck deep.

Nose—

Evil yanked.

Chapter Twenty-One

AMPED TO THE MAX

EVIL'S CONSCIOUSNESS snapped back into his own head. Disorientation made him stumbled back and someone kept him from falling.

Though free, Evil's mind insisted that he was blind from the darkness, his body was numb from the darkness, and the air that came through his gasping mouth was the darkness spilling down his throat and into his lungs.

He was drowning. Still.

His physical senses tried to compete with what his mind wanted to believe, but their input of muffled gunfire, stinky air, and hands holding him didn't compare to the reality imposed upon him by Tar.

Whoever held him up from behind let go as two people grabbed him from the front and shook him. Slapped him—

The slap stung. His skin wasn't numb.

They shook him again.

He was able to see again and what he saw was another hand too close to dodge or block.

Slap!

Four-Arms was in front of him. She held his wrists at his

sides with her lower arms, her upper right hand held his left shoulder, and her upper left arm cocked back in preparation to slap him again.

Behind her, Demon's formerly white-fire eyes were pools of inky black as he stood in a stupor.

Evil said, "I'm good." He pulled his wrists from her hands and shielded his face. "Stop slapping me."

Four-Arms released his shoulder.

Wide-eyed, Evil rubbed his stinging cheek as he looked around to verify that he was, indeed, back in the prison.

The reality of the gashes on his chest pulsed pain through his torso.

Evil knew that real-world time moved much slower than time during a psychic intrusion, but the drowning numbness of Tar's trap had robbed his short-term memory of his situation.

Some of it came back in snatches.

Demon's claws had done a number on him and he wasn't hearing because of something Pilgrim did to his powers.

Grasping his chest and rocking in place, Evil remembered everything through seeing Bunyan's fall, but the rest—The rest felt lost. Lost somewhere beyond his reach.

He said, "Deborah?" Why had he said that name?

"Deborah?" Four-Arms shook her head. "My name's Kimiko."

"Huh?" Evil blinked away his confusion and said, "Not what I meant." He remembered the Deborah he absorbed years ago and that she was what was rebelling against Pauly. And she wasn't in him anymore. At least, Evil didn't feel her apprehension about Demon being twenty feet away.

Four-Arms said, "I thought you guys had regeneration."

Lupe said, "They do." Her voice came from behind him.

Evil turned to look—

He grimaced and stopped. Twisting doubled the pain from the cuts. He groaned.

Lupe said, "Pilgrim sapped his powers. Regressed them back to when they first manifested."

"Oh." Four-Arms' expression changed to a problem-fixing smirk. "Why didn't you just say so." She grabbed onto Evil's shoulders and wrists.

Evil tried to move away. Four hands on him from one person was weird and the angle at which her lower hands had ahold of his wrists was unnatural.

The pupils in Four-Arms' brown irises shrank to a needlepoint, and then expanded to nearly fill her irises.

Evil gasped as her pupils opened. That body-thrumming amped-up feeling resonated through his being. His powers came roaring back, smashing through his normal levels and dialing everything up to the point where Evil felt like they would burst out of him.

Sounding rushed, Lupe said, "Kimiko. He's good. Now do me. Let's get back home."

Four-Arms released Evil and said, "Girl, you better not screw me over again."

Drunk with power, Evil stumbled forward as the pain in his chest lessened. The wounds rapidly closed before his eyes. It was like he was watching his own regeneration at ten times speed.

He'd been empowered before, but what Four-Arms was able to do was unprecedented, and that was with her nullifier collar on.

Amazed and unable to figure it out, Evil said, "Your powers must be off the charts."

Taking ahold of Lupe as she had Evil, Four-Arms glanced back at him.

Evil's telepathy picked up her surface thoughts, *Only in this dimension.*

He didn't mean to do that, but his power was dialed beyond his normal control. Lupe's thoughts were there too, and held his attention.

Kimiko is going to flip out if I can't make the jump. She'll probably kill me. I really hope Ev chooses to help me.

Evil asked, "Help you what?"

Lupe glared at him and, in Four-Arms' grip, she began to shake uncontrollably.

Four-Arms released Lupe. "You're up."

Lupe said, "I need—" With a little more grace, Lupe stumbled around like Evil had. "I need you—" Lupe gasped and laughed as she looked at her hands and body. *I'm totally juiced!*

Feeling similar, Evil asked, "Need me to what?"

"Help." Lupe turned her attention to him and tapped her forehead. "I need you to go in here and help me envision home." As though admitting something painful, she bit her lip before summoning the courage to continue.

Lupe admitted, "I've been here so long that I've sort of forgotten what *home* looks like."

When Lupe said *home*, Evil felt her longing desire to be back where she was from. To see if her real parents were still alive, to get back to a dimension where the world couldn't be held hostage by one powerful ultrahuman and his offspring. A dimension where heroes embodied the standards that both powered and non-powered people strived to live up to.

While a lot of what she thought of her home dimension was probably colored with the broad strokes of Lupe's younger self, the part about not being held hostage stood out. Any child in this dimension knew who Supreme was. Evil's great-grandfather had carved out a chunk of Mexico and the US to call his own and was able to hold it for decades. American textbooks call Supreme a terrorist turned world leader.

Also in Lupe's speaking *home*, Evil could envision a smattering of tall trees—oaks and firs—on a wide, gently sloping hill of wide, deep green grass that dipped out of view, and the sounds of a babbling brook.

His telepathy and empathy formed an image in his mind of what she called home. Evil projected the image into her head.

He said, "Does this look familiar?"

Tears welled in Lupe's eyes. "Yes."

Evil said, "Focus on it."

Lupe closed her eyes and did. A wide smile spread her lips as a ten-foot pyramid of air behind her began to shimmer. Like in the mental image, tall trees and a field of grass could be heard through the shimmering, Also, the faint sound of a flowing stream.

Four-Arms said, "You did it, Loop." She rushed through the shimmering, onto the grass.

As she crossed over, Demon fell limp.

Four-Arms danced in joy.

Lupe opened her eyes, turned, and squealed. "Thank you." It looked like she was going to spring a hug on him, but restrained herself. "Thank you."

Lupe ran toward the portal.

The asphalt split. A wall of earth blocked her path to the portal.

Speaking Spanish, his great-grandfather Supreme's strong mental voice filled the area. "Miss Lupe Carvalho."

Lupe looked completely different. For a moment, Evil wondered how he knew this woman was Lupe and then remembered the lesson his father gave him about mental signatures.

Supreme asked, "Have you forgotten the oath you swore to my country?"

Evil felt the proximity. Supreme had arrived.

Chapter Twenty-Two

NOT SO SUPREME

BESIDES RELATIVE STRENGTH, Evil's TA never warned him of his family's actions. He'd learned that with his fight with his father. However, he realized for the first time that Supreme's mental voice didn't feel like it was going to smother him or crowd him out of his own head.

When Evil turned, Supreme stood there in a redesigned forest-green and black field military uniform. His black flat-top patrol cap on his head was as black as his skin and the symbol of Primazone, a snake with the wings, beak, and talons of a golden eagle was stitched at the center in silver thread.

Lupe's voice went quiet. She kneeled and answered in Spanish. "Of course not, Supreme Overlord."

"Good. Because—" Supreme scrunched up his nose and turned to Bunyan's body, which was creating the smell. Reddish-purple energy surrounded him as Supreme used his telekinesis to lift himself into the sky to look down upon the big guy. Somber, he said, "This man is supposed to be dead."

"I know." Evil naturally switched to Spanish just as he naturally—when actually in his great-grandfather's presence—

thought of his great-grandfather as Supreme. "Surprised me, too."

With Supreme's mental voice not being overwhelmingly strong, Evil tried to bring the conversation back to Lupe leaving, and lied, "She's still loyal to Primazone."

"Really." From Supreme, the lone word never sounded like a question. Then again, with a cabal of precogs feeding him the future, there probably wasn't much he didn't already know. It was only the well-kept secretive nature of this prison that kept it from being discovered before now. If Supreme had allowed his precogs to scan along his lifeline, he would've seen this coming, but then they'd also be able to plot against him.

However, Evil's lie wasn't challenged. Something his father and Supreme regularly did instantly to him.

Supreme took ahold of Bunyan with his telekinesis and lifted the big man from the ground. He asked, "Then why didn't she alert the Network as soon as she discovered you?"

Lupe said, "I—"

"For—" Evil spoke over her. Her lies as to why she didn't send up some signal to the telepaths and precogs of their county would stand out like an albino. "—the same reason Pilgrim didn't. They didn't know it was me until a little bit ago and she was over there on the other side of Bunyan."

"Bunyan?" Supreme nodded as he started to slowly lift Bunyan into the sky. "Yes, that's his name." Bunyan went above the buildings as Supreme asked, "And how could they not know you? You, the power-soaked crown prince of Primazone?"

Another lie not challenged. Being amped up must've broken whatever method Supreme had of catching Evil not telling the truth.

"Nullifiers." Evil pointed to metal around Lupe's neck and motioned to Pilgrim. "Mine was quite powerful and the signature color of our skin wasn't apparent." Evil glanced up to Bunyan, a good hundred feet in the air and rising.

Supreme said, "Really."

Evil said, "Yes." He started to feel out the wall Supreme had pull up in front of the portal. It was just desert hardpan. His own earth control had always been weak, but amped, he worked to start hollowing the wall by pushing the center back down into the earth.

Supreme glanced from Bunyan to them. "Rise." He gave Lupe permission to stand as he turned his attention back to pushing Bunyan higher. "They have nullification technology that surpasses our own?"

Evil thought about seeing his natural skin tone again. He stopped on the wall and sent the image to Supreme.

Bunyan's ascent stopped as Supreme turned and asked, "Really?"

Solemn, Evil nodded. He did his best not to glance at Bunyan, nearly two hundred feet from the ground. That was the usual execution height to which Supreme lifted the powerless or absorbed ultrahumans he was going to execute. If Evil did look at Bunyan, Supreme would return to lifting Bunyan and then let him go.

Bunyan's weight was nothing to Supreme's telekinesis. Lifting him slowly like that must've been a personal pleasure or fulfilling a personal grudge.

Supreme's gaze went from Evil to the buildings. He narrowed his eyes in concentration. His gaze went to the antennas and then back to Evil. "Can you see into the building or pull the metal from them?"

Still working on the wall, Evil shook his head as though he had tried and found the task impossible. He was pretty sure there wasn't any actual metal in the building, but he wasn't going to offer that info.

Knowing better than to press a conversation while

Supreme was thinking, calculating, Evil waited. His eyes flicked to Bunyan. Crap.

"No matter." Supreme turned his attention back to Bunyan and, while lifting him higher, pushed the big man sideways so that he would be over one of the southern buildings. "Think two hundred feet would be enough for him? No." Supreme answered his rhetorical question. "For the same results on his body size, we'll need to go to fifteen hundred. Should be higher for the ratio of his size, but a body at terminal velocity is a body at terminal velocity. Right?"

"Right." Evil answered like he was supposed to. He then angled to getting Lupe permission to leave. "Supreme, she recognized my voice. Advised Pilgrim, and Pilgrim dissolved my collar so the Network could detect me. The pure loyalty deserves to be rewarded with a vacation to a countryside before returning back to duty."

"Is this true, Miss Carvalho?" Supreme kept lifting Bunyan, but turned to face them. "Did you really recognize the crown prince's voice?"

Crap. Evil's hope of getting her free sank. She was going to lie and Supreme was going to see through her. And, since it was a direct question to her, Evil wasn't supposed to say a word.

Don't lie, Lupe. Evil didn't send the thought to her for fear that Supreme would intercept it, but he hoped really hard. *Don't. Lie.*

Chapter Twenty-Three

THE SUPREME RULE

LUPE LOOKED up to where Supreme was, but—as she was supposed to—didn't make eye contact and kept her gaze below Supreme's chin.

Without Bunyan near them, the air went from the burnt smell of the big man's body back to nasty burnt sox. The gunshots slowed, and besides Pilgrim in an ice ball, they were alone in the large yard.

Lupe said, "I didn't recognize him by his voice."

"No?" Supreme turned his attention to Evil. Accusation began to heat his eyes.

Lupe continued, "That's what he may think, but I recognized his face. And I always will."

Supreme's eyes cooled as he returned his attention to her. "But you are not to look directly at the crown prince, Miss Carvalho. How do you know his face?"

Lupe said, "We went to school together for years before we turned ten and that rule was implemented. He has a tiny mole beneath his lips and another on the side of his neck."

Evil's empathy picked up on Lupe's emotions as she was speaking. He knew fondness and reverence well. However, what she felt for him was like those combined, but deeper and—when she mentioned his moles—attraction laced into the other feeling.

Knowing how she felt made Evil feel uncomfortable. Not the fact that she had that feeling for him, but that he knew how she felt. Today had been full of first times, and him feeling like a creep for knowing was another. He locked onto her mental signature and added it to the short list of emotions not to casually observe.

Evil's old crush on her rekindled and he felt emotionally naked.

"Ahhh." Supreme gave a rare smile. "I see." He glanced appreciatively between the two of them. He asked Evil, "And, least to say, you would like to go with her on this... vacation?"

Evil answered. "Yes, great-grandfather." He hadn't called Supreme that since he was ten, but it felt right. Sort of how the idea of being in another dimension felt right; he'd be free from his legacy and all the trappings that came with it. "If you'll allow it. But if not, I will return to Ultrava with you."

Supreme's lip curled up as he thought it over. He then looked at Lupe and a flash of reddish-purple energy, a mental probe, shot from him to Lupe. Supreme's eyes widened in rage.

Evil collapsed the wall. He shoved Lupe with his telekinesis. No more victims. His legacy was his burden.

Lupe stumbled through. The portal closed.

At least one of them would be free.

"She's gone!" Supreme turned his enraged stare upon Evil. "She's nowhere on the planet."

Evil said, "She said she was going home."

"Did you know?" Supreme's reddish-purple mental energy spread toward Evil like a sentient cloud of vapor. "Tell me true. I don't want to see otherwise."

"No." Evil found Tar's trap anchored in his mind and

bolstered it. In case his plan didn't work and the fortified trap wasn't strong enough to snag Supreme, he obscured the fact. Then, as though he didn't know about the trap, he spread his arms and pretended to open his mind.

Evil said, "Look and see."

Supreme's mental cloud closed in, formed tendrils in front of Evil's eyes, and dissipated. Supreme said, "I trust you." He extended his hand. "The royal teleporter is waiting to bring us home, great-grandson. We need to get above the antennas."

The supreme ruler of Primazone was not fond of familiar references. So, his using one softened Evil's heart toward his great-grandfather.

Supreme said, "We shall marshal our forces, show that you are safe, and then return. We'll peer into the minds of those who work here to find all involved, find where they live, find their families, and exact our vengeance by snuffing them all out."

"Uh..." Evil hesitated at grabbing Supreme's hand.

Distant yelling, Bunyan yelling, caught Evil's attention and he looked up.

Bunyan was awake way up there and his massive lungs carried his calls for help.

Supreme's telekinesis holding the big man up faded. He said, "We'll start with him."

Bunyan plummeted toward earth. Bellowing.

Evil's gazed tracked him as he fell.

According to his father's teachings, Bunyan deserved to die because he aligned himself against the family and then against Primazone. A sentence punishable by death and being carried out.

Supreme nodded and turned. "Yes, let's watch."

Evil grabbed ahold of Bunyan with his telekinesis, strained for a moment, and stopped the big man from falling to his death. Evil rapidly brought Bunyan down to the roof and dropped him ten feet from the building.

Bunyan landed and shrank to be out of view.

Supreme rounded on Evil. "You saved that ultra. Either you kill him or his punishment is upon your shoulders."

Evil summoned his mental shields. "That ultra did nothing wrong."

"Nothing wrong? Not that you know of." Dismayed, Supreme shook his head. "You have worked against me twice and do not understand your folly." A cloud of mental energy swirled into tendrils around Supreme's head. "Looks like I'm going to have to put you in stasis with your father until you learn."

Evil gritted his teeth, balled his fist, and prepared psionically charged cryoblasts. "Or I free the world from your tyrannical reign."

Chapter Twenty-Four

BATTLING SUPREME

SUPREME BALLED HIS FIST. Pillars of earth shot up through the blacktop, knocking Evil into the air.

Evil activated his flight. He made a telekinetic bubble around himself. He shot a blast at Supreme.

Supreme's telekinetic shield stopped the physical ice, but the psionic blast hit. He winced like he had looked into a spotlight.

Evil release his next shot.

This time Supreme's shield stopped both. Supreme shot a spear of mental energy.

Evil dodged. His telekinetic bubbled burst.

Evil made another bubble.

The furious mental energy skimming by felt physically hot. Which wasn't possible, unless—

Supreme's next spear burst the bubble.

It struck Evil's shoulder, knocking him in a backward spiral. His flesh seared. His brain warmed.

Supreme had laced the psychic attack with fire.

Evil formed another bubble and reinforced it with mental shields.

Supreme shot again.

As though made of glass, the bolt shattered against the bubble. Shards of mental energy exploded away from Evil like fiery coal shrapnel.

Evil shot his own cryo-enhanced mental spear.

It broke through Supreme's telekinetic barrier. It drove into his gut.

Supreme's eyes flew wide open. He bellowed, "Impossible!"

Evil launched another and another.

Supreme got a barrier up before each, but it wasn't enough. Both spears found their mark. Supreme's midsection was now encased with ice. He started to lift himself up.

Evil put a telekinetic ceiling above Supreme to keep him from getting above the antennas. To keep him from getting away.

Yelling his exertion and might, Supreme powered up a foot.

Evil growled as he stopped the rise.

And started.

To shove.

Supreme.

Down.

Again, Supreme yelled, "Impossible!" His cap fell off revealing wispy hair. He relented to the force and summoned two spears.

Evil closed in on Supreme as he slammed him against the asphalt. He was doing it. He was winning.

Supreme shot both spears at the same time.

One missed Evil. The other shattered off of his bubble.

Some of the fiery mental shrapnel landed on Demon. Who twitched, but remained unconscious.

Evil pinned Supreme to the blacktop.

Dozens of columns of earth shot up at Evil at the same time.

Evil weakened them with his own earth control as they came. His bubble held strong.

The columns broke open like useless clods of dirt; debris rained.

Evil said, "Yield."

"Never!" Supreme ground his teeth. He pressed up.

Evil bit hard and pushed down. "Yield!"

Then his powers begin to wane. He glanced at Pilgrim.

The ice around the man had mostly melted. Only his lower body was held from the knees down. Keeping his balance, Pilgrim waggled those power-sapping fingers at Evil.

Evil shot cryo at Pilgrim and put him back on ice.

Supreme pressed up.

Evil pressed down.

Supreme started. To get. Up.

Slowly at first, then with greater ease.

Evil tried harder to force him down. No good.

Supreme sneered at Evil just like his father used to. "Somehow, you were stronger than me, but loyalty and tactics always win out." Supreme closed his hands in the air as though he could physically grab Evil's bubbled at a distance. And his telekinesis did.

Pilgrim had weakened Evil so much that the reddish-purple of Supreme's mental energy was barely visible.

The pressure building up on Evil's bubble quickly became too much. Noting the force matched Supreme's hands, Evil let the bubble burst, popping him down between the gap in crushing force as Supreme clapped.

Evil caught himself a foot from the wrecked ground. He lifted himself to be five feet above the tilled and destroyed asphalt.

His TA told him he was outclassed.

Something he already knew.

It told him to run.

Something he was already considering.

"You are my blood." Supreme crossed his arms and lifted himself to be ten feet above the earth to look down at Evil. "I take no joy in this."

Evil disagreed. "You do. It's why you took on the name Supreme, because you can't help but proving that you are better than other ultras."

"Perhaps." Supreme formed another mental spear. His telekinesis grabbed ahold of Evil to keep him still. "Until we see each other again, any parting words?"

Growing tall on a southern building, Bunyan threw a vest —Evil's nullification vest—to the ground. He then leapt at Supreme.

Supreme spun, caught Bunyan in the air, and flung him up into the sky. He spoke English as his mental voice carried the message up to the man rocketing upward. "I paid to have you killed, friend." Supreme reveled in watching Bunyan sail high into the sky. "Again, I have to do things myself."

Evil lifted the vest with his telekinesis and flapped it onto a gloating Supreme. He fastened it.

Supreme's skin lightened to gray and his mental energy instantly became visible again. Better yet, the reddish-purple color was very rich, signaling Supreme's weakened state.

Evil's TA told him he had a chance again. He grabbed Supreme and slammed him back to the ground.

Supreme made an earthen dome around himself.

Leaving the physical dirt structure untouched, Evil locked onto Supreme's mental signature and hit him with a ferocious psionic attack. And another.

Supreme's consciousness flicked and faded.

A riotous scream came from high up.

Evil searched for the source.

Bunyan was coming down fast.

Evil tried to stop Bunyan with his telekinesis at a thousand feet.

Velocity forced the man through.

Evil grabbed onto Bunyan's torso at eight hundred feet. He pulled up.

Seven hundred feet.

No appreciable difference in speed.

Six hundred feet.

Evil kept struggling and projected to Bunyan, *Shrink!*

Five hundred feet.

Bunyan shrank, but terminal velocity for more mass had been hit. Still pulling, Evil struggled.

Four hundred feet.

There wasn't enough space.

Three hundred feet.

Evil made a telekinetic ramp.

Two hundred feet.

And pulled Bunyan to it.

One hundred feet.

Evil lost hold of Bunyan when he hit the ramp at the top where the slope was gentle.

Bunyan tumbled out of control down the widening slope like an amusement park car coming down a blind drop.

Evil pushed on Bunyan with Deborah's air control.

Bunyan didn't slow in the least, but went all the way down the ramp and bopped clear across the prison yard like a tumbleweed in a windstorm. He grew to full size and the increased mass slowed some. Not enough to stop, but enough to merely cause great damage to the northern building instead of being a bloody splotch on it.

Supreme's mental signature flew up.

Evil spun and shot a psionic blast.

Knocked unconscious again, Supreme went limp and started to fall.

Evil caught him, took a deep breath, and let out a long sigh of relief. He and Bunyan had done the impossible, but what now?

Chapter Twenty-Five

WHAT IS BEST

HOLDING his unconscious great-grandfather aloft with his telekinesis, Evil took a look around.

The asphalt that had been smooth and perfect a few hours ago now had gigantic chunks ripped up and turned over. The jutting blacktop and earth looked like someone had whacked a pie with a sledgehammer. Surprisingly, only one building had been damaged and only two bodies: Supreme and Demon.

Usually, when Supreme went someplace outside of his country, nearly all the buildings were leveled and many bodies littered the wreckage.

Evil set his great-grandfather down on a rare patch of undamaged blacktop.

The area looked bad; the smell of freshly turned earth was a much-welcomed change from the musky stench that hung in the air. Evil used his air control to blow out the earthen smell and bring what he thought would be fresh air from further up. But the tinge of spent gunpowder that was up there was now down here.

A few more shots from the guns reported.

Evil became aware of the sound of his ragged breathing. Trying to calm himself, he took deep steady breaths. In, and out. His stress, his turmoil, started to ease.

In, and out.

Evil hit Supreme with another psionic blast to make sure he'd remain unconscious. His father had a telepathic trick to keep someone unconscious, but Evil had left before he could learn it. Logically, it was probably steadily supplying a low amount of telepathic might, but occasional blasts would have to do for now.

He looked up at the antennas.

If the royal teleporter sent Supreme here, any number of other ultrahumans could be showing up as soon as they started to think that their leader was gone for too long. It wouldn't be too soon, because Supreme hated to be interrupted, but they would come.

For a moment, Evil thought about sneaking the body to the stasis chamber where his father had shown him his grandfather, but he had no idea how the machine worked. Worse, if anyone ever checked in on it, they would see both elder Overlords on ice.

Bunyan came tromping over. The weight of his steps lightened as he shrank from being fifty feet tall to being twelve. The big man had a grip of collars—six or seven—in his hands. He knelt and put one on Supreme.

The gray of his skin lightened.

Bunyan put on another.

Supreme's skin turned the same color Evil's had been when he had been fully nullified.

Bunyan said, "Can't believe I'm seeing this."

"Me either." Evil was equally amazed. While seeing his own skin tone return seemed right and natural, it looked super weird on his great-grandfather.

Still astonished, Bunyan shook his head, gave a small laugh, and said, "This happened. You did it."

"We did it." Evil said that more in reaction than thought. While he believed in sharing credit, that *we did it* felt more like trying to share the responsibility for accidentally breaking something.

And something was broken. His family bonds.

After this, there'd be no way Supreme would forgive him, and if his great-grandfather ever got free, Evil knew he'd be at the top of the hit list. Just thinking about the possible future made him want to run and hide.

Bunyan said, "The whole world is going to breathe easier."

Evil screeched, "No." Bunyan didn't know about the precogs. As soon as word of this hit the air in the future, they'd be backtracking other future events to find the soonest moment that they could rescue their leader.

Bunyan asked, "*No?* What do you mean, *no?*"

"Yeah." Evil nodded. "No. No one can know about this, Bunyan. In fact, you probably should take my great-grandfather and go into hiding."

"As if." Bunyan scoffed, "Why would I do that instead of helping the world relax?"

It didn't feel right revealing everything, but the big man had to have a reason. Though they had close to fifty, Evil said, "We have a well-paid and well-cared-for precog in the Primazone whose sole purpose is scanning future news events. I don't know how far out she can see, but once this gets reported, you can bet everything you'll ever have that the Primazone elite will go into action the moment she reports it. She *will* report it and they *will* come for him."

"Well." Bunyan stood. "We have special facilities here. We could put him down in the deep cells."

Evil said, "No."

"And why not?"

"Because." Evil pointed up to the antennas. "Those may keep teleporters from porting in here, but my great-grandfather's royal teleporter sent him here." He waved a hand around the general area where his great-grandfather had appeared. "Where do you think the search party will be sent?"

"I get it." Bunyan nodded. "Yeah, I get it."

Evil said, "If you have another facility like this, or can build one, take him there."

Bunyan nodded.

Evil pointed to the collar and asked, "Can I get a couple of those?"

Suddenly leery, Bunyan handed him two.

Evil went to Demon and slapped one of them around the muscular, deep purple neck. The musclebound demonic body shrank down to mostly being Pauly, but with lavender-skin.

He pointed to his great-grandfather and said, "Wherever you take him, Pauly—" Evil corrected himself, "Paul Gantt here should go there, too."

Bunyan frowned, "Why?"

Putting the second one on, Evil asked, "You mean besides being an entirely out of control demonic ultrahuman?" Evil didn't want to get into the split personality bit with the bad one being in charge. Any telepath worth their salt would discover that. "Well, he's also a wife-beater. And I mean bad."

Something in Bunyan's unchanged expression told Evil that the big man doubted that.

Evil said, "Tell you what, have your telepaths probe his mind to back when he was married to a blue-eyed, blonde-haired, tan-skinned ultra named Deborah. Have them go to when she discovered she could fly and the path of abuse will be laid out forward and backward."

Half-heartedly, Bunyan said, "Okay."

"Seriously." Evil insisted. "It's there. It might be years old, but he did it and if you guys came after me when I did nothing, you should definitely check him out."

More certain, Bunyan nodded and asked, "And what about you? Are you going to stay here?"

Evil shook his head. "I don't belong here. What did I do to deserve prison?"

Bunyan's eyes searched the air for an answer. He shrugged and asked, "Then what are you going to do?"

Evil took a deep breath. "Well, first would be to wear one of those—" Evil pointed to the remaining collars in Bunyan's hand. "Until I can get another vest."

Bunyan handed one over.

Evil put it on. His skin lightened to gray. He continued, "And then go back to my life, I guess. I mean, you guys will know where I am and I'm okay with that."

"That's not going to happen." Bunyan frowned. "We can't let you go back to your act of being Ernest Smith Jr. when we know the guy is being held for ransom somewhere out there."

"Well..." Evil bobbed his head. He had let Bunyan in on the precog secret, might as well tell him one more. "What if I told you that he was in on it?"

"On what? On his own ransoming?"

Evil nodded. "Well, sort of. It's not a ransom thing so much as it's a you-take-my-place-so-I-can-party kind of thing."

Bunyan asked, "How could I trust you on any of this?"

"I could have Ernest call you, but—" Evil pointed at the voluntary collar that he had just put on and motioned to Supreme. "Need I say more?"

Bunyan sill looked doubtful.

"What?" Evil couldn't believe it. Bunyan still clung to him not being free. Evil asked, "You think this is a plot?"

Bunyan gave an uncertain nod. "You guys are known for this kind of thing."

"Oh. My. God!" Evil puffed. "To what end?"

"I don't know." Bunyan shrugged. "To know about the secret prison?"

"Really?" Evil laughed. "Really?" He didn't mean to, but he had. "To highlight how ludicrous that is, here are some of the moving parts." Evil grabbed his index finger. "One, I pretend to run away from my home country where I was a *ruler* years ago to work at a coffee shop." He grabbed both his index and middle finger together. "Two, also pretending, my dad puts an end to all—let me repeat that, *ALL*—pure Chinese to really kill my mother to—"

"That was to kill your mom?" Bunyan's eyes widened like the universe had told him a secret. "We—We never knew why he targeted Chinese people."

"Yeah." The thought of his mother being gone because of his father stole some of Evil steam. He swallowed. "Well, now you know. And if you think you have anything here that is worth a billon lives, then you could be right. You wouldn't be, but..." Evil heaved a sigh. This had grown beyond tiresome.

Bunyan asked, "So, you'd just go back to work?"

"Yup." Evil nodded. "That's what I was doing before and that's what I'll go back to. I'm happy with a simple life."

Bunyan asked, "What about a GPS tracker?"

Evil shrugged, "Everyone else in America has one, why wouldn't I?"

"Okay." Bunyan extended his hand. "Deal."

Appreciative, Evil shook Bunyan's hand. "Deal."

Chapter Twenty-Six

NO NEED TO HIDE ANYMORE

STANDING JUST inside the back door at Norwest Grind, Evil set the two large bags of garbage down from the four p.m trash. He reached under his shirt and rotated the nullification dial three soft clicks that he felt more than heard, which took the vest from a nine point five down to an eight.

Being able to adjust the nullification setting on the vest was just one of the few already implemented ideas that he had given to Jimmy after his ordeal last month. If he set the vest at ten, he'd be totally nerfed, and eight was the lowest he could go without any difference to his skin tone.

The genius was still working on integrating other ideas, but another feature Evil was glad to have was a safety phrase. In case he was restrained, he could deactivate the vest with words alone. The best thing about the new vest was that he didn't have to pretend to be Ernest. He was now Juan Garcia, an exchange student the Smiths were sponsoring.

Evil picked the trash back up. With a bit of his ultrahuman strength returned, the bags were easy to handle. He could easily handle them both with one hand, but didn't.

He elbowed the door release and stepped down into the back alley.

The sound of traffic motoring beyond the employee parking was steady. He hadn't noticed the lull when Granite and Brown Mist surprised him last month. Now he paid attention again and didn't let daily common things go unnoticed.

As organized as always, all the stores had their pallets and garbage bins tucked tight to the walls. The League had paid for the damage done to both the garbage bins and the wall last month.

He lifted the garbage bin lid and the smell of spoiled milk puffed out. Holding his breath, Evil shook his head, tossed the trash, and closed the lid. Apparently, training wasn't going to be the solution to the milk and cream carton problem.

He stepped away from the bin's stink and contemplated solutions. His first thought about having a separate bin for the dairy containers was interrupted by his TA signaling a potential threat at the mouth of the alley.

Pretending that he was turned to just be going back into the building, Evil glanced toward the potential threat. His TA put the woman at 5'4". She was slim and the largest threats on her body were her hands, her skin, and her forehead. The sunlit parking lot behind her made it hard to see who she was.

Evil asked her, "Can I help you?"

"Maybe." The woman's voice was quite girly. "I'm looking for Ernest."

Evil said, "He's not due back until next Monday."

"Well." She stepped into the alley. The potential threat, the fact that she had powers, stayed as just a potential. Nothing active. She presented a business card. "Could you give this to him?"

"Sure." Evil took it. She studied his face as he read *Guadalupe Carvalho. Relocator.*

She said, "Is that you Ev?"

Evil asked, "Lupe?"

"Yes." She smiled. "I finally found the one you worked at." She pointed at his face and hair. "I thought you were, you know, incognito."

Evil smiled back. "Well, without power-soaked skin, no one recognizes me—and why would they, right? It's not like anyone ever had a chance to get to know my face before."

She nodded. "So, no need for a falseface anymore."

"Nope." Evil grinned and put the card in his pocket. She was still studying his face. He cleared his throat. "Uh, so, what's up?"

Lupe said, "Kimiko has finally gotten around to forgiving me for accidently getting us to this dimension. And I saw a news special where I'm from about the son of a hero who didn't want to be a hero, and it sort of reminded me of you."

Evil nodded slowly. "I could see that."

"Anyway." Lupe's smile was constant. "Seeing how you're not into world domination and the heroes here won't leave you alone, I figured I would give you the option of leaving this dimension and coming to mine. Our dimension just got powers fifteen years ago, there are more heroes, and no powered individuals have taken over countries."

"Wow." If Evil had had this option a month ago, he would've leapt at it. "Wow." Now things were sort of cool. "I don't know what to say. Thank you—"

"Great!" She bubbled. "Do you need to get anything?"

Evil scratched his neck. "Actually, I wasn't finished." He looked elsewhere in the alley and then at her. "Thank you, but things are okay now."

"Oh." Lupe's smile waned.

"I mean." Evil sighed. "I made a couple of deals here and I wouldn't want to up and disappear on them."

Her smile was gone and her understanding nods were looking more and more forced.

Evil took ahold of her hand. "But if I had the power, I'd definitely come visit you."

Lupe asked, "You would?"

"Yes." Hoping she'd smile too, Evil smiled widely.

She joined him.

Glad, Evil said, "But I don't, so you'll have to come visit me. How often can you use your power and is there any downtime?"

Lupe said, "After I use it, it takes me twelve hours before I feel like I can do it again."

Evil said, "Hold on. I'm going to go get a couple of scones and we can go talk in the park."

Lupe said, "Okay."

A few minutes later, they were sitting on a bench at the city park. Evil watched Lupe's face as she excitedly told him about what had happened in her dimension since she had returned.

While he updated her, it occurred to him that he was casually eating in a park with a girl he liked. He didn't have to have a falseface on and didn't have a single worry in the world.

Things were really going to be okay.

THE END

Ezekiel would like to give thanks to:
Colleen Kuehne
John Young
Kari Kilgore

ABOUT THE AUTHOR

Ezekiel James Boston hales from Las Vegas and currently resides in the Pacific Northwest. Favoring fantasy, science fiction, and paranormal occult, he's authored over a hundred short stories, a score of short novels, and half a dozen full length novels.

Aside from being an avid writer, Ezekiel enjoys reading and games of all sorts. He chose to give up "active" sports after jamming his fingers and discovering that an author cannot slam their forehead onto the keyboard and have the story appear on the screen.

For exclusive content, please visit:

ezekieljamesboston.com/subscribe-to-ejb/

ALSO BY EZEKIEL JAMES BOSTON

Benjamin Baxter Novels:

Birthday Bedlam: Book One

Samhain Shenanigans: Book Two

Yuletide Yield: Book Three

Novelette:

Nexus Bar & Grill: A World of Benjamin Baxter Starwise Novelette

Short stories:

Gateway Blood, Buck Tales

Soul Survivor, Buck Tales

Jamal & the Skeleton's Heart, Buck Tales

Collections:

Benjamin Baxter — Darkness Within Trilogy

COMING SOON

VANGUARDS, Ultrahumans #2

IMBOLIC INSANITY, Adventures of Benjamin Baxter Book Four

WELCOME TO FLOWERLAND, A Novel

PLEASE NOTE: Word of mouth is crucial for any author to succeed. If you enjoyed this book, please consider rating it or leaving a review where you purchased... Even if it's just a line or two.

Thank you for reading.

www.ingramcontent.com/pod-product-compliance
Lightning Source LLC
Chambersburg PA
CBHW030349200626
46808CB00022B/834

* 9 7 8 1 6 2 5 3 8 0 5 2 4 *